It can't be me," he whispered, streaks of blood punctuating each word, splashing back up into his face to trickle through his neatly trimmed goatee.

Why in all the planes would this thing come to kill him? He'd made it a point, as his father always advised, to steer clear of wizards, gnomes, and other dangerous types. He kept his dalliances discreet and was careful to avoid women with jealous husbands or protective brothers.
As he ran through the tall-ceilinged maze of his family's city house, he couldn't think of anything he'd ever seen like the horror that was chasing him, and there was no reason for it, though …

… though he wasn't the only one.

**From the creators of the
greatest roleplaying game ever
come tales of heroes fighting
monsters with magic!**

By T.H. Lain

The Savage Caves

The Living Dead

Oath of Nerull

City of Fire

The Bloody Eye

Treachery's Wake

Plague of Ice

The Sundered Arms

Return of the Damned

The Death Ray

T.H. Lain

THE DEATH RAY

©2003 Wizards of the Coast, Inc.

Distributed in the United States by Holtzbrinck Publishing. Distributed in Canada by Fenn Ltd.

Distributed to the hobby, toy, and comic trade in the United States and Canada by regional distributors.

Distributed worldwide by Wizards of the Coast, Inc. and regional distributors.

Printed in the U.S.A.

Cover art by Todd Lockwood & Wayne Reynolds
First Printing: October 2003
Library of Congress Catalog Card Number: 2003100843

9 8 7 6 5 4 3 2 1

US ISBN: 0-7869-3030-6
UK ISBN: 0-7869-3031-4
620-17992-001-EN

U.S., CANADA,
ASIA, PACIFIC, & LATIN AMERICA
Wizards of the Coast, Inc.
P.O. Box 707
Renton, WA 98057-0707
+1-800-324-6496

EUROPEAN HEADQUARTERS
Wizards of the Coast, Belgium
T Hofveld 6d
1702 Groot-Bijgaarden
Belgium
+322 467 3360

Visit our web site at www.wizards.com

For Gary Gygax & Dave Arneson,

with thanks for all this.

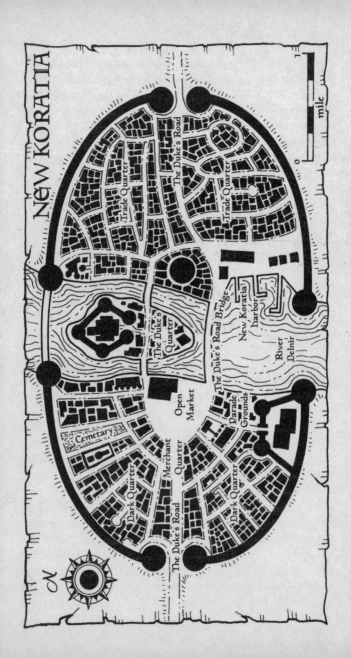

NEW KORATIA

Trade Quarter

The Duke's Road

Trade Quarter

New Koratia harbor

The Duke's Road Bridge

River Delnir

Cemetary

The Duke's Quarter

Merchant Quarter

Open Market

Parade Grounds

Dark Quarter

The Duke's Road

Dark Quarter

mile

0

N

Prologue ... He closed his eyes just before his chin hit the cold marble floor, smashing his teeth together and cracking at least one tooth. His hands, numb at the ends of shaking, flailing arms followed soon after, though he'd meant for them to hit the floor first and save the teeth. Thick, hot, coppery blood covered his tongue. When he opened his mouth to draw a deep breath into protesting lungs, he coughed, sending a spray of blood and chips of teeth fanning across the floor in front of him.

"Get up," he grunted to himself, trying to ignore the terrified quaver in his voice. "For Fharlanghn's sake, get up and run!"

He got to his feet, stumbled once, then ran. His knees shook so badly he could make barely half the speed he knew he was capable of, and the rhythmic shudder of the floor didn't help. His racing, terrified mind went back and forth between the urge to run faster and the need to sacrifice some speed in order not to fall again.

The floor shuddered again, and a dull boom rippled through the high-ceilinged hall. The memory of a brief glimpse of the behemoth chasing him was all he needed to make his legs finally move faster. The air tossed his long, clean hair behind him as he ran, moving alternately through shadow, candlelight, shadow, and candlelight as he passed the gilded sconces set along the walls.

He coughed again. Blood dribbled from his chin and onto his expensive, silk tunic. The rapier tapping against his left leg as he ran was more a piece of jewelry than a weapon, and he had no illusions about either its strength or his own swordsmanship. The thing chasing him would surely snap the fine blade like a dried twig.

He passed the huge, double doors that closed off his parents' private suite and kept running. He knew no one would be there. The house was empty, save for a skeleton staff of servants and maybe half a dozen guards who he was sure were already dead. The family was gone to the country for the warm summer months, when the smells of the Trade Quarter grew strong enough to fight the prevailing winds and descend upon the collection of fine manor homes on the Duke's Island.

Though he remembered insisting that he stay behind, as he ran through the grave-quiet corridors, the heavy air disturbed only by those thunderous footsteps, he couldn't recall why. There was a girl or two in the winding alleys of the Merchant's Quarter, to be sure but he couldn't have been willing to sacrifice himself for any of them.

Of course, he'd had no idea an enormous, heavy-footed monster would come to kill him.

"It can't be me," he whispered, streaks of blood punctuating each word, splashing back up into his face to trickle through his neatly trimmed goatee.

Why in all the planes would this thing come to kill him? He'd made it a point, as his father always advised, to steer clear of wizards, gnomes, and other dangerous types. He kept his dalliances discreet and was careful to avoid women with jealous husbands or protective brothers. As he ran through the tall-ceilinged maze of his family's city house, he couldn't think of anything he'd ever seen like the horror that was chasing him, and there was no reason for it, though …

… though he wasn't the only one.

"Gods," he breathed as the thought came to him.

There was a door hanging ajar and he slid to a stop in front of it—overshot it actually but he stumbled back to slip into the chamber beyond. It was his father's library.

As he crossed the wide room at a run, he recalled the news of the past few weeks. Young men, men he'd known his whole life, from important families, had been found dead. There were as many "official" causes of death as there were rumors. His family had left before the first of them was killed. They didn't know—none of them knew—that there would be any danger. Could the other young men have been chased down and murdered by this thing? To what purpose?

He came to the foot of a wrought iron staircase and tripped again as he stumbled up the first few steps. Catching himself, he ignored the bruising shock to his forearms and scurried up the stairs, cringing at every step as his boots clanged on the delicate latticework.

His father's library was four stories tall, a huge gallery easily seventy feet in height. The stained glass ceiling looked dull under the midnight sky but in the daylight it was the envy of the finest families in New Koratia. Imposing bookcases lined all four walls with galleries circling each level. There was only one way into the room—the way he'd come—and only one way up. The wrought iron staircases matched the railings that circled the galleries. He used the railings to pull himself along, grasping for an opportunity to put distance between himself and those horrid, stomping footsteps.

He would be trapping himself in the upper reaches of the gallery, he knew, but it was the only place he could think of to hide. The thing chasing him would be too heavy to climb the stairs and too big to fit between the tight rows of heavy bookcases made even heavier by the thousands of books jammed onto them. If he could get high enough up and deep enough into the library, he could hide long enough to think of something—perhaps long enough for help to arrive or for the thing to tire and go away.

The booming sounds came more quickly, almost on top of one another, and increasingly loud. It was moving faster and getting closer.

More from panic than from any sort of plan, he made for the fourth, uppermost gallery. There, the room widened again, and the bookcases were arranged in rows barely two feet wide. The bookcases themselves were solidly made of the sturdiest hardwood. Packed as they were with books, scrolls, and manuscripts of every description and in myriad languages, they were as heavy as brick walls.

He reached the second set of stairs and was certain that the booming footsteps had come around the corner of the corridor outside. At that rate his pursuer would be at the door before he stepped onto the third flight of steps.

"Get there!" he urged himself, more loudly than he'd intended.

The tingling in his mouth had become a throbbing ache, broken only by razor stabs of pain as his heavy breathing pulled cool air over broken teeth. He tried not to imagine how much worse the pain would be when the thing finally had him, when the injuries were worse than a blow to the jaw. The thing was big enough to crush him and likely strong enough to tear him limb from limb.

That thought was, thankfully, interrupted by the realization that the footsteps had passed the door.

He didn't stop, barely even slowed, even as that potentially life-saving fact dawned on him. He reached the third flight of stairs with a smile, laughed halfway up, but then his blood ran cold. The footsteps behind had stopped. The tower was quiet—easily quiet enough to hear someone running up a flight of wrought iron stairs, laughing.

There was a boom, then another—louder, closer—and it was at the door.

He made it to the uppermost gallery and dodged behind a huge bookcase that soared eight feet over his head. From below came the sound of the library door being ripped from its hinges, then the first booming footstep echoed in the confines of the library itself.

He turned a corner, already lost in the maze of bookcases. The floor beneath his feet trembled through a rapid series of footsteps. His shoulder clipped the edge of a wood-bound manuscript that protruded from a low shelf, and he grunted as he spun to a flailing, bruising stop on the hard floor.

He managed not to hit his head but he thought he had when his teeth and eyes and tongue vibrated in his skull. It wasn't the fall that made the deafening, skull-shaking sound. Something huge, something as heavy as a caravan cart, had hit the floor.

The sound came again, then again, then again, and as he stood, hoping to run deeper into the maze of shelves, the bookcase to his left was peeled off the floor and thrown into the air.

He screamed but the sound was swallowed up by the crash of the bookcase shattering on the floor atop four others. Looking up into the eyes of the behemoth, he had just enough time to whisper a prayer before he died.

Regdar felt like a new man. Out of his heavy armor for what seemed like the first time in years, he even felt lighter. He'd been to a barber in the morning so his hair was neatly trimmed, his face cleanly shaven, and he'd had a bath. Pressed for time, he'd stopped short of a leeching. He had something to pick up at the shop of a master bowyer.

Naull had picked out the gray tunic of light wool that he wore and the matching breeches. Though far from fancy, the outfit was new, clean, and quickly tailored to fit his bulging physique. The shoes bothered him, though. They were also chosen by the pretty young mage who had become his constant companion in the weeks since they returned to the city from the frontier keep. The shoes were too low and too soft. They were city shoes, more appropriate for polished marble floors than his old boots. In that respect they were probably a good choice but they still made Regdar nervous.

He walked briskly, and alone, down the entrance hall of the duke's palace. Regdar felt like he was walking down the middle of a deep canyon. The walls soared so high over his head, he was only dimly aware of being inside at all. The intricately decorated flying buttresses seemed altogether too tall to have been made by humans, though indeed they were. The light seemed to radiate from the air itself—not too bright, not too dim. Even Regdar recognized that particular touch as decidedly magical.

At the end of the hall he came to a set of double doors that surely could have accommodated the shoulder width and headroom of a storm giant. In front of the door were two guards dressed in ceremonial armor, their azure tabards embroidered with gold thread in the house arms of the Duke of Koratia. The spindly dragon design was as familiar to Regdar as his own face. The same device was painted on his shield, though his dragon was red against gold—the field colors of the Comitatus. Each of the guards held a wickedly-bladed halberd. The polearms and their armor all but vibrated with magic. Regdar let slip an impressed smile. Those guards were hardly to be trifled with, however frilly their dress.

The big fighter was also aware of several other sets of eyes on him, though he couldn't be certain of their exact hiding places. To be sure, more than two men guarded the door to the duke's palace, and Regdar suspected it would require ten times that many simply to pull open the mighty doors.

When he approached within half a dozen steps of the guards, one of them said, "State your name and your business before the Duke of Koratia."

The man's deep voice didn't echo in the huge hall. It seemed to drift over Regdar with an air of perfect, calm authority.

"I am Regdar," he answered, "late of the Third New Koratia Comitatus, Red Dragon Regiment, here at the request of His Highness the Duke."

By the look on the guard's face it was obvious to Regdar that the man knew exactly who Regdar was and why he was there. Without answering, the guard stepped to the side, as did his companion. The doors swung slowly inward. Neither of the guards had touched them, and the great golden hinges made no sound. When they'd opened more than enough to allow Regdar to pass, the guards bowed slightly and Regdar stepped through.

The entrance hall had been impressive but the chamber within was awe-inspiring. The ceiling soared to an impossible height, and everywhere were frescoes and gilding and bas relief. Regdar thought it would take months, perhaps years, for him to study every work of art for more than a few seconds. The floor was the same polished marble as the columns, buttresses, and ceiling. The masonry was so fine that if Redgar hadn't believed it impossible, he might have thought the entire room was cut from a single slab of stone covering an acre of land.

Regdar saw the duke, surrounded as usual by a small crowd of palace advisors and bodyguards. The duke noticed Regdar, too, but continued speaking with his retainers, not watching as Regdar closed the imposing distance between them. The big fighter stopped a few yards short of the assembly and stood, strictly out of habit, at attention.

The duke finally turned his piercing green eyes on Regdar and smiled.

"You may stand at ease, footman," the duke joked.

Regdar felt his face flush and he took some uncomfortable effort in trying to be casual. Noting his discomfort, the duke stepped up to Regdar and clapped a hand on his shoulder.

"Regdar," he said, "old friend. Have you been enjoying the city?"

"Yes, Your Highness," Regdar replied.

"And still I can't bother you with staying at the palace?"

"No," Regdar said, too quickly. He winced, cleared his throat, and added, "Respectfully, Your Highness, no, thank you, but the inn you recommended is already more than I require. I have simple needs."

The duke gave Regdar a devilish, teasing wink and clapped his shoulder again.

"A thousand pardons, Your Highness," a lithe elf said, stepping out of the crowd of faceless advisors. He held a slate and a delicate stylus. Glowing runes on the slate gave the elf's face a pale blue cast. "The appropriations, Your Highness?"

"Will have to wait, Minister Nyslorvijiik," the duke replied, not bothering to look at the elf. Instead, he pressed gently but firmly against Regdar's shoulder, leading him away from the ministers.

"But—" the elf started.

The duke stopped, turned to the elf, and leveled a cool, silent gaze at him. Minister Nyslorvijiik went a bit pale—more embarrassed than afraid—and he sketched a quick bow.

"As you wish, My Duke," he said, taking two steps backward.

Duke Christo Ramas was as tall as Regdar, and though a good thirty years the fighter's senior, he was still a strong, solidly built man. A full head of wavy, white hair and an equally colorless beard framed his time- and stress-worn face. His hands, rough and scarred, were a warrior's hands. The ring finger of his left hand was missing. Regdar had heard more different stories of how the duke sustained that injury than even the most talented bard would have been able to recall. His dress was as simple as Regdar's, though azure where the fighter's was gray.

The duke led Regdar a few steps farther into the room, and the fighter could hear the others backing away as well, giving them more room.

"I am glad to see you, my young friend," the duke said. His voice was quiet, conversational, but still commanding.

"You flatter me, Your Highness," Regdar replied.

The duke chuckled and said, "I will admit to anyone who will listen that I was more alive, and more a leader, against the janni than I've ever felt here. It is an honor to lead this duchy, to be certain, but the true honor lies in the command of men such as yourself."

"I am a soldier," Regdar said. "I serve."

"Yes," the duke said, his voice and manner growing even lighter, perhaps wistful. "You serve. You serve indeed, and are a soldier forged of the finest steel, my friend, but you could be more."

"More, Highness?"

The duke stepped closer—uncomfortably close—and held Regdar's eyes with his own.

"A man," the duke said, "the right man, could rise as high as . . ."

With a sigh the duke looked away, then down at the floor, as embarrassed as the interrupting minister had been. Regdar felt his face flush again and he, too, looked away.

"I get ahead of myself," the duke said, "again."

A series of staccato clicks sounded on the marble floor and Regdar's eyes were drawn to their source. The duke also looked up to see a beautiful, young woman approaching with long tendrils of silk wafting behind her in a delicate wake. She was wrapped in silk that clung to her slim curves in an almost uncomfortably alluring way. Walking straight and tall, she slipped across the floor in elaborately braided sandals that, from the sound they made, were surely fitted with taps. Her hair was the color of hay and even the gruff fighter knew its gentle curls had been painstakingly arranged to fall just so over one delicately arching eyebrow. Certainly still in her teens, the girl's face betrayed a singular self-confidence beyond her years. Her crystal green eyes were of a set with the duke's. In a way Regdar felt as if he was looking at a smaller, younger, softer version of Christo Ramas.

"Ah," the duke said, breaking the silence, "Maelani."

The girl smiled and fluttered to a stop before the two men.

"Father," she said, dipping into a shallow curtsy.

"Regdar," the duke said, touching the fighter on the arm, "late of the Third New Koratia Comitatus, and a good friend."

The girl smiled, showing straight teeth of almost blinding white, and said, "Regdar. . . ."

"My daughter," the duke continued, "the Lady Maelani."

Regdar bowed, feeling a bit on display under the girl's embarrassingly precise gaze.

"My lady," he said.

"My father has told me a great deal about you, Regdar," Maelani said. "Your efforts in defense of the duchy are . . ."

She seemed to be searching for a word, and the duke said, "Most appreciated."

Maelani's cheeks flushed red and she looked away.

The duke laughed and said, "My daughter studies well and often, and will soon enough comport herself like the duchess she's destined to be."

Maelani either couldn't or didn't bother disguising the irritation in her face.

"She's lovely," Regdar broke in. His face flushed red with embarrassment, and sweat trickled down his chest.

The comment that Regdar so regretted made the duke laugh and Maelani blush again. She smiled at the fighter, who looked away.

"I'm sorry, Your Highness . . . L-lady . . ." Regdar stammered.

"Surely you've heard that my daughter's hand is the most sought-after prize in the duchy, if not the world," the duke said, and again Maelani showed her irritation. "She is reaching the age where a marriage is possible, and I am reaching an age where her marriage is necessary. She is my only child, Regdar, and I love her deeply. She is also my only heir, and I love Koratia at least as much . . . though in a different way," he added hastily.

Regdar nodded, still too embarrassed to follow what the duke was trying to say.

"Maelani," the duke said, "I would suspect that we'll be seeing more of Regdar in the coming weeks. I hope that prospect pleases you."

Maelani, whose future husband would eventually become the Duke of Koratia, smiled and nodded. Regdar began slowly to understand. He felt the color drain from his face, and his forehead went damp and cold. His mouth was dry. He tried to clear his throat but instead made an unbecoming, weak, squeaking noise.

Surely, he thought, the duke remembers Naull and everything I went through to get her back.

"It does please me," the beautiful young woman replied with undisguised pleasure. "I would like to hear of your worldly experiences . . ."

Regdar's jaw went slack and he had to blink sweat out of his eyes.

"With the Comitatus, of course," Maelani added.

Regdar sagged with relief.

Though he wasn't the tallest of men, Vargussel's spiky hair
brushed the rafters of the dark passageway. It was the easiest
of prayers to Vecna that caused the tip of his staff to glow like a
torch. Without it, he would have stumbled around in whatever
inconsequential twilight seeped through the crumbling roof of
the abandoned slaughterhouse. As it was, it was difficult enough
to avoid the many deep puddles of fetid, vile water. Vargussel's
long, green robe was already spattered with muck that obscured
the wine-red trim around the hem.

The place was cool but humid, and sweat beaded on his forehead as he picked his way deeper into the dilapidated building. The
corridors were designed for cattle, not men. When the place was
abandoned decades ago, no one bothered to clean it. The smell was
a constant reminder of how low Vargussel had been forced to sink
at times in order to inevitably rise so much higher.

Vargussel breathed through his mouth, quickening his step so
that he would reach his hiding place deep in the old slaughterhouse
before he was overcome by the stench. Sweat collected on his chest
and back, under the heavy, quilted tabard in a wine-red diamond
pattern mimicking the heraldry of his family. It was an old pattern

for an old family—a family that would die with Vargussel if he failed in the coming days, but he would not fail. For his family, all gone but him; for his liege, still waiting and watching from afar, he would—

Vargussel stopped. His foot splashed in a puddle of syrupy muck that slid over the top of his fine leather boot. Something was wrong. Something was different. Vargussel had come to the old slaughter-house often enough, for long enough, that he could feel the change in the air.

He wasn't alone.

In front of him was an intersection, one he'd crossed a hundred times. He was a few long strides from the intersecting passage, so he couldn't see around the corners. The ceiling was a bit higher there, the walls close enough on either side that Vargussel could have reached out and touched both walls at the same time. There was no change in the heavy stench of decay. He heard no sound but the odd drip of water and the creak of an old gate hanging from one rusted hinge. The intersections had once been gated so the butchers could heard their charges in one direction or another. The other three gates were missing, long gone.

With his glowing staff still held in his right hand, Vargussel slipped two fingers of his left into a pocket of his robe. There he found a small bead of blue glass, a spell focus he carried, along with many others, everywhere he went. He didn't pull the bead from his pocket but just held it and whispered the brief incantation while closing his eyes in the precise way the spell demanded.

Without opening his eyes again, he could see. The lighting was different, more diffuse. His perspective was changed slightly, as if he'd suddenly become a few inches shorter. Concentrating on steady, even breaths, Vargussel altered his perspective by sheer force of will. Without actually moving a step—he stood stock still, his eyes still closed—he moved his sight forward, up, and around the corner to the right.

The spell showed him the dark expanse of the narrow side passage. Scanning it briefly, lingering on the ceiling, he saw nothing.

The shadows were deep, however, and Vargussel wasn't entirely convinced that the passage was clear. Before risking the time to move his sight deeper into the right-hand passage, Vargussel willed his perspective to turn, then slide back to the intersection. He caught a brief glimpse of himself with the magical light on the end of his staff illuminating the crumbling brick, rotting wood, and stagnant mud around him.

He moved his sight into the left-hand passage. When he tilted it up to scan the ceiling, he saw something move.

It was a twitch, really, a shadow expanding itself in an unnatural way. He moved in a bit closer and could see the outline of something clinging to the dark corner where the sagging ceiling met the cracked wall. The thing was vaguely humanoid but skinny. It's elongated arms were more like tentacles and at the end of them dangled grotesque, five-fingered hands that, seen only in shadow, looked more like squids than hands. The thing shifted its head around and twitched its shoulders. It was becoming restless, probably wondering why Vargussel had stopped.

Vargussel let the spell effect fade to darkness. When he opened his eyes, he saw through them normally once again. He touched the medallion hanging from a heavy chain around his neck. It was small enough to fit in the palm of his hand. The medallion was shaped vaguely like the head of a dog, with a long snout simply rendered and two large rubies where its oblong eyes would be. Letting out a small, silent breath, Vargussel willed the guardian to come.

Still standing in the same place, Vargussel took his hand away and whispered a quick spell that would protect him—at least a little—in the meantime. It was a minor casting, but wasting it and the clairvoyance was testing his patience. The fact that the Vecna-given light on the end of his staff would burn out half an hour after he cast it gave him a sense of irritated urgency. Still, Vargussel wasn't the type to let an opportunity pass.

"Come out," he said, his voice echoing in the tight space.

Somewhere, a flock of pigeons, startled by the sudden sound of a human voice in the dull silence, took wing. The thing in the darkness around the corner stirred as well but didn't reveal itself.

"I saw you there, my friend," Vargussel said. "A clever hiding place indeed, but you've been found out. Come down and speak with me, and perhaps we can avoid all this nastiness I'm sure you had planned for me—and that I've been planning for you as well."

There was a long silence during which Vargussel considered how to kill the thing if it didn't come down. As if sensing his line of thought, the thing in the corner came out.

It unfolded itself slowly, almost gracefully, like a worm coming out of an apple. It clung to the upper corner of the passage, holding onto a rafter beam with its left hand. Its webbed feet splayed out on the wall and seemed to hold it there like suction cups.

"That's it," Vargussel said, keeping his voice light, unthreatening. "Come down, and introduce yourself like a gentleman."

The thing slid off the wall, making a horrid, wet, sucking sound when its feet came loose. It splashed into a puddle of reeking muck without flinching from either the cold or the smell. Vargussel moved his staff in front of him a few inches and the light fell over the creature.

Its eyes closed against the light and its skin wrinkled around its small, deep-set black orbs but it didn't back away. It might have stood only four feet tall, if it stood erect, but it didn't. The slight creature crouched, not cowering, in front of Vargussel. Naked, its skin looked like burnished steel gone splotchy with rust. The flesh of its long legs and arms was smooth but elsewhere it was wrinkled and sagging, even where it hung from deeply-cut ribs. Its head was narrow, with a high forehead and pronounced jaws. As it stared at Vargussel, it's lipless mouth slid open to reveal two rows of vicious, yellow fangs, each as long as one of Vargussel's fingers.

"Well, then," Vargussel said, "there you are."

"No fear me, human?" the creature said, it's voice high but still menacing.

Vargussel smiled politely and said, "I do not fear a lone choker, but thank you for asking."

The choker, as Vargussel had identified it, was a wretched vermin that would lie in wait for unsuspecting passersby, then squeeze the life out of them. It opened its eyes a bit wider and tipped its head.

"Yes," Vargussel said, "I know what you are."

"How know?" the choker asked. "Why here?"

"I know a great many things," Vargussel replied. "As to why I'm here, that is none of your concern. Suffice it to say that I have laid claim to this dismal ruin for reasons of my own. It is you who is the trespasser."

"No understand," the choker hissed. "Who you?"

Vargussel was about to answer when the floor quivered under his feet. The choker twitched, startled, looking around, and Vargussel knew the creature had felt it too.

"Pay that no mind," Vargussel said. "A storm is coming . . . thunder and all that."

The choker tipped its head again and nodded.

"Who you?" it asked again.

"I am Vargussel, but you can call me Your Highness."

"Highness?"

"I intend to be duke," Vargussel replied. "By marriage, mind you, but duke just the same. Do you know what that is . . . a duke?"

The little humanoid shook its head, and its long, tentacle-like arms twitched.

"Well," Vargussel explained, "it is a title that identifies a man of great importance—a man it might do you well to serve."

"Serve you?" the choker surmised, its eyes narrowing again.

"Serve me," Vargussel said.

The choker's right arm shot out toward Vargussel's face like the snatching tongue of a tree frog. Grotesque, wormlike fingers splayed open, reaching for Vargussel's throat to grasp it in a palm lined with jagged spikes. It meant to strangle him, not serve him.

Vargussel didn't flinch, didn't move, and the hand stopped short, no more than an inch from his neck. The man lifted an eyebrow and looked into the darkness behind the choker, where something enormous loomed.

"Wrong answer," Vargussel said, and the choker was snatched backward.

The creature whimpered, then coughed out a sound that might have been a bark. Vargussel stepped forward and held his staff out and up. Light poured over a massive form of steel and wood and glinted off eyes of thumb-sized rubies. It revealed on the thing's chest a duplicate of Vargussel's amulet, and likewise illuminated the shocked, terrified face of the little choker.

The shield guardian—Vargussel's shield guardian—had a hold on the choker. The steel fingers of its left hand wrapped around the creature's slim torso. The choker's arms whipped back in a feeble attempt to ensnare the guardian, but the huge construct, sitting on its knees in the confines of the passage, paid it no mind.

Vargussel shrugged and stepped past, moving around the two creatures as best he could. He came close enough that the choker saw him. Its tentacle arms snapped back into place, then made to reach out again. The shield guardian drove the choker into the wall hard enough to dislodge a ceiling beam.

Vargussel stepped away from the falling dust and blood. The choker squealed, and the shield guardian drew back its right arm, pausing to let Vargussel pass. When its master was out of the way, it curled its metal fingers into a fist the size of a man's head and smashed it into the choker's skull. The creature's neck snapped and one of its black eyes careened into the air only to splash into a puddle of decades-old cow dung.

"So that was the whole reason you were summoned to the palace?" Naull asked over the shiny silver teacup.

Regdar sighed, shrugged, and didn't bother to answer. Naull shook her head, then sipped her tea, and Regdar looked away.

Absently, Regdar's hands fiddled with the collapsing bow he'd purchased early that morning. It was expensive, but when he saw it he knew he needed to have it. How much easier would it be to carry a bow that folded into a slim leather satchel than the long composite bow that had gotten in his way so many times while slung over his shoulder and dragging on the ground?

They sat at a small table on the huge, high terrace of the Thrush and the Jay—the inn that the duke himself had recommended to them—sipping tea from wildly expensive silver cups and taking in the cool, sunset air. Regdar had never stayed in a place so opulent before. Almost everything about the inn made him feel silly, like a fish out of water.

Naull, who grew up in a lonely wizard's tower on the eastern frontier, was oddly at ease. The beauty and elegance of the inn seemed to transform her, bringing out a grace that Regdar had always sensed in her but hadn't often been able to see. She was a gifted spellcaster with a quick mind and an easy wit. Surrounded by silver, silk, and servants, she became a lady.

Naull set down her teacup and met Regdar's eyes. He smiled when he realized he'd been caught staring at her when he'd meant to look away.

"She must be very beautiful," Naull said, a smile curling her lips.

Regdar shrugged and this time did look away, out to the east where the pale orange glow of the sunset held the city in its gentle embrace. From where they sat, high atop the columned inn, the Duke's Quarter stretched out beneath them with the eastern portion of the Merchant's Quarter behind it and the bustling Trade Quarter beyond.

"More beautiful than a poor country wizard, anyway," Naull mused.

Regdar ignored the comment and lifted his teacup to his lips. His huge hand engulfed the delicate, silver vessel in a most uncouth fashion, but the fighter didn't care. He let his eyes wander the city, which was a great oval surrounded by mighty walls. Those walls were well maintained, even washed regularly on the duke's orders so that their polished, gray-white stone glowed in the warm light. The River Delnir cut through the heart of the city, flowing from the north on its way to the endless expanse of the Southern Sea some dozen miles away.

The Thrush and the Jay occupied a large and expensive tract of real estate right on the western strand and the terrace overlooked the fast-flowing river. Orange light glittered on the water where the inn's shadow didn't fall. Directly across was the Duke's Quarter, an island in the middle of the river. The duke's palace towered over them, stretching over the entire northern half of the island. Surrounded by brilliant white walls of its own, capped with a cluster of soaring towers, the palace was easily half a mile on a side.

A coach that appeared to be cut from solid gold, pulled by a team of white horses and flanked by a dozen of the duke's elite guard, rumbled over the bridge that linked the island with the Merchant

Quarter. The coach and its outriders disappeared from sight below the rim of the terrace to pass along the south wall of the inn.

"She's smart, too, I suppose," Naull sighed.

Regdar, engrossed with the view of New Koratia, barely heard her. A flash of light caught his eye and he squinted at the Floating Crystal. The renowned college of wizards was an enormous, floating tower of glass. Though it was almost a mile away, it still appeared huge, hovering over the wizard's reserve on the eastern side of the river. Behind it, the labyrinthine streets of the Trade Quarter formed a backdrop of chaotic shapes. Beyond that he could see the twin towers of the east gate.

"She's had tutors," Naull continued, "to teach her everything, perhaps even to school her in the most exotic and secret lore of love and pleasure."

Regdar's attention returned to her abruptly, and her eyes flared.

"That caught your attention?" she asked, arching an eyebrow at him.

He took a hasty sip of tea and flinched in surprise when he found his cup empty. He set the cup down on the lace tablecloth and shifted in his too-small, wrought iron chair.

"So you were introduced," Naull said. "Then what?"

"That was all," Regdar replied, studying his silver teacup.

"More tea?" Naull asked, reaching for the pot.

Regdar grabbed it before she could, though, and drew it toward him.

"I've got it," he said.

"Yes," she said, her voice dripping with sarcasm, "I'm sure you do."

"What's that supposed to mean?" Regdar found himself asking, against his better judgment.

"Oh, you know what I mean," she replied, looking away and sighing.

"No," Regdar said, "I don't. You're angry with me because I accepted an invitation from the Duke of Koratia himself?"

She turned on him and Regdar almost flinched at the fire in her eyes. He had no doubts about Naull, but had to force himself to understand that she could be angry, even with him, and it was a sign of nothing but her humanity. Considering her recent past, all they'd both been through, Regdar doubted she'd be offended if he occasionally watched her just a little too closely.

Naull folded her arms across her chest and started tapping her foot.

"What have I done?" Regdar asked.

The fighter was suddenly aware of other eyes on him and he looked up. The waiter, a lanky weasel of a man wearing a floor-length tunic in the ubiquitous blue-gray of the Thrush and the Jay, was standing next to their table.

"My apologies for interrupting," the waiter said in an accent Regdar couldn't place. "Is the tea to your liking?"

Regdar looked down at the empty tea cup, realized he was still holding the pot in his hand, and said, "Fine, yes."

"My lady?" the waiter asked, bowing in Naull's direction.

"Lovely," the young woman said, plastering a smile on her face for the waiter's benefit.

The waiter bowed lower and turned on his heel, the clean white towel draped over his left forearm flapping lightly in his own breeze.

Before he could take a step away from them, Naull said, "No, wait."

Like a soldier snapping to attention before a general, the weasely man turned back to Naull and bowed again.

"Lady?" he asked.

"I have a question," Naull said, sitting up straight in her chair. The fine silk of her dress and the finer wool of the sweater that she wore over her shoulders against the cool evening air whispered on the wrought iron. "If someone were to introduce you to a young lady, and—oh, I'm sorry, are you married?"

The waiter went pale, swallowed once, and said, "Yes, my lady."

"Naull . . ." Regdar cautioned, setting the teapot down without pouring himself another cup.

The young mage paid him no mind, focussing instead on the waiter.

"If someone were to introduce you to a young lady," she continued, "having made some effort to exclude your wife from the meeting, then was careful to inform you that the young lady was in need of a husband and that you would be someone she'd be seeing more of . . . what would you think?"

The waiter swallowed again and looked around, as if expecting a hoard of demons to appear from the thin air and rip him to pieces.

You should be so lucky, Regdar thought. Both of us should be.

The waiter cleared his throat and said, "A scone, perhaps?"

"No," Naull said, "thank you. What would you think?"

"I'm sure I have no idea what—" the waiter began.

"Of course you do," Naull interrupted. "You would think that, regardless of your wife, dutifully waiting at home for you, washing your blue-gray tunics, feeding your children, serving you in bed like a—"

"Naull!" Regdar blurted.

"Ma'am!" the waiter squealed at the same time.

Naull ignored them both and continued, "You'd think he was trying to arrange a marriage, wouldn't you? Do you love your wife?"

The waiter took a step backward as if slapped by the questions. Regdar sucked in a breath, looked around, and saw a good dozen sets of eyes directed at their table, at the little parlor drama Naull insisted on playing out. The other diners were the finest people of New Koratia, and Regdar doubted they'd ever seen anything like the shameful display.

"Do you?" Naull pressed.

"Naull," Regdar stage-whispered, "for Pelor's sake."

She held up a hand to silence him and lifted an eyebrow at the waiter.

"I . . . I do," the poor man said, swallowing again.

"And you would tell this match-maker, however well meaning," Naull went on, "that you love your wife, you honor your vows, and have no interest in marrying this home-wrecking little trollop of his."

The waiter blushed and said, "Yes?"

And that was when Regdar said exactly the wrong thing: "But, we're not married."

"Get those clothes off," Maelani ordered as she slipped off her own delicate shoes.

"Mistress!" her young maid hissed, her cheeks turning red, her hand coming to her chest to cover her heart.

Maelani ignored her. She pulled back the curtains enough to stick her face out of the open window of her coach.

"Driver," the duke's daughter said, "we'll wait here for Theria. I will be napping and will expect not to be disturbed."

"As you wish, My Lady," the driver answered.

Maelani closed first the glass window, then the curtains, so that the interior of the coach was plunged into a perfumed grayness. Her maid hadn't started taking off her clothes.

"I said strip, damn you," Maelani whispered.

Theria began opening the catches on her humble servants' gown, worry turning quickly to panic on her chubby, round face.

"Oh, Mistress," the young girl murmured, "oh, dear. Don't make me do this."

"For Cuthbert's sake, Theria," Maelani replied as she quickly unlaced her own corset, "stop whining and do as I say."

A tear slipped down the maid's pudgy cheek, but she continued disrobing. Maelani did the same and handed her own garment of fine silk and wool to her maid, then collected Theria's less expensive—and less obvious—clothes on the seat next to her.

Soon, the two young women were wearing each others' clothes and though Theria had stopped crying, she was no less beside herself.

"Mistress," she squeaked, "please let me go in your stead. Please don't go out there ... oh, Pelor ... oh, Pelor protect us all if something were to happen to y—"

The maid squealed when her mistress's warm, soft hand clamped over her mouth like a vise.

The duke's daughter leaned in close and whispered, "Shut your thrice-bedamned mouth, will you? I told the driver I would be taking a nap. You're me, so for all the gods' sakes, will you please take a nap?"

Maelani took her hand away from the frightened maid's mouth and pulled on her simple, homespun cloak.

"Oh, Mistress ..." the maid started again.

"Nap," Maelani hissed. "Will you take a nap?"

"But Mistress," the maid persisted.

Maelani pulled the cowl over her head, shielding her face from view, and said, "Will you please just take a nap. Will you? Please, just take a nap."

"But Mis—"

"Take a nap!"

The maid clamped her own hand over her mouth and shut her eyes tightly. Tears oozed from the corners of her eyelids but she made no sound.

"I will be back when my business is finished," Maelani said. "In the meantime, make no noise, open no curtains, and for Cuthbert's sake don't speak to anyone. The driver and the guards won't disturb you if they think you're me, and they think you're sleeping. Sleep if you want to, or just sit there with your hand over your mouth, but wait for me in complete silence. Do you understand?"

Theria nodded and Maelani, opening the door only as far as she needed to, slipped out of the coach.

Without looking at the driver, or the escort of a dozen guards who sat on their horses in front of and behind the gilded coach, Maelani dipped her head and set off along the well-swept sidewalk, heading north. The coach was parked across the street from the front entrance of the Thrush and the Jay, New Koratian society's most oft-visited inn. It wouldn't be unusual at all to see Lady Maelani's coach parked there. The shops across the street were among the finest in the city, and she was seen shopping there often.

Disguised as she was in her maid's common clothes, Maelani easily slipped into the flow of foot-traffic following the street northward to the first side street. There she turned left, heading east along a street that curved gently to the south, following the contour of the city wall that rose half a mile to her right. On her left hand was the bustling Merchant's Quarter, on her right, the finer establishments slowly faded into the mazelike sprawl of the Dark Quarter. Maelani knew her father would die of heartstop if he knew she was so close to the Dark Quarter—the city's crime-ridden slums—but he didn't need to know, and she was confident that her simple ruse would work well enough that he never would.

Still keeping her head down and her cowl closed tightly over her face, she passed the rolling hills and marble-studded expanse of the city's cemetery. At the second major street after the cemetery, she turned right, moving into the very edge of the Dark Quarter.

Though the sun was rapidly setting and the shadows growing ever deeper around her as the crowds thinned and the streets became more rugged, dirtier, and more rank, she was not afraid. She'd gone this way more than once, and wealth and station were not without its privileges, even in disguise. The magical trinkets her father insisted she wear would protect her, she was sure, long enough for her to flee at least back into the relative safety of the Merchant's Quarter should something go awry.

Soon she saw the imposing ruin of the Slithraan estate. The ample, walled-in land and the jagged towers of the manor house were out of place there, a relic of a time when this part of the city was home to a better class of people. The surrounding mansions were torn down decades before, some even moved brick by brick to the island or the eastern shore of the river. Only that one manor was left, standing like a decaying reminder of the city's—and her father's—hypocrisy. No effort was made to clean up the Dark Quarter, just contain it, keep it away from the better people and keep the better people away from it.

Well, Maelani thought, this better person goes where she pleases.

She approached a much more modest, single story house directly across the street from the crumbling estate and went quickly to the door. The paint was peeling from the wood, and there were holes and a spot of fresher color where a knocker used to be. A dim glow flickered in the windows but no sound came from within. Maelani reached up to rap her delicate knuckles against the door but didn't quite manage to touch it when she was startled by a sudden click, then a squeak, and the door swung inward on its own.

The space inside was close, crowded with furniture that smelled as old as it looked. A big, old, gray cat sauntered past, paying her no mind as it twisted itself between a forest of chair and table legs. A single candle burned on a tabletop, wax dripping onto the peeling surface. Behind it sat a woman.

"Vrilanda," Maelani whispered, stepping into the house.

The woman smiled, keeping her lips together, and brushed back her long, curly hair to reveal a pointed ear. Her eyes were a pale silver—a color Maelani had never seen in a human's eyes. Vrilanda, of course, was no human. Though her house and the furniture in it were entirely human-made and gave one the impression that the resident was surely of great age, Vrilanda appeared as young as Maelani, though the duke's daughter knew the elf was old indeed, by human standards.

"My Lady," Vrilanda said, her voice ringing with the musical accent of the elves, "come in, sit down, and tell me what you wish of me."

Maelani stepped in, deftly avoiding another cat that gave her an impatient glance as it wandered past. The door swung shut behind her and locked itself with a sharp click that made Maelani jump.

Vrilanda smiled wider, revealing perfect white teeth. She indicated a chair across the table from her. Maelani sat, resting her arms on the rough service of the old table.

"I need a potion," the duke's daughter said.

The elf's smile faded, but not all the way, and she asked, "You have alchemists in the palace, do you not?"

Maelani sighed and said, "You know why I'm here. No one must suspect . . ."

She stopped, surprised at herself for being embarrassed to tell Vrilanda exactly what she needed, why she needed it, who she needed it for, and why no one must ever know of it.

"You need a . . . potion?" the elf witch prompted.

Maelani nodded, then met Vrilanda's gaze.

The duke's daughter took a deep breath and, blushing, said, "A love potion."

It was as much the vibration as the sound that shook Regdar
from a deep sleep. The low rumble was followed by a clatter of wood
that might have been a windblown shutter.

He opened his eyes but saw only the vague outlines of the
big, canopied bed, the black shadows of the room's heavy, antique
furniture, and the faint bluish glow that crept in under the thick
curtains. The whisper of Naull's soft skin on the satin sheets was
enough to erase the memory of the sleep-disturbing rumble.

His eyes adjusted to the darkness enough for him to see that
Naull was turned toward him. The bedclothes were pulled up just
enough to expose the soft glow of her bare shoulder. They had
fought, though Regdar still wasn't sure why, and they had made
up, and again he wasn't sure why.

Regdar slid the covers up to his own chest, ignoring the chill in
the air. Under the covers, he could feel the warmth of Naull's body
next to his, then the soft caress of her breath on his cheek.

"Regdar?" she whispered.

He reached out and pressed his big palm gently against the side
of her face. She responded by moving closer to him, letting his huge
arm drape itself around her slim shoulders.

"It's all right," Regdar whispered. "It's just a storm."

Already asleep, Naull whispered, "Storm ..." and melted into him.

Regdar closed his eyes, letting the warmth of her body wash over him, feeling what remained of the tension of the uncomfortable evening dissipate into the warm, perfect darkness under the covers with the woman he loved.

In a room just down the hall, at about the same time, Serge d'Allion was startled awake. He knew instantly what had roused him. He'd cast a spell before retiring, one that would silently alert him if anyone entered the room.

Though both the security and the discretion of the Thrush and the Jay were near legendary in New Koratia, Serge was a careful sort. His dalliances were of no concern to his parents. He was twenty years old, certainly of an age where he could bed whom he pleased. Still, certain things were expected of the heir to the d'Allion fortunes, and his parents were nothing if not traditional. If he was found out, he would be disowned. He could lose everything.

Serge sat up, letting the cool satin sheets fall from his bare chest. The door was ajar, and in the dimness he could make out the form of Zhellian, the young elf he'd come to the Thrush and the Jay to spend a secret night with.

"Where are you going?" he asked, keeping his voice low so as to draw no attention in the quiet inn.

The heavy curtains blew around the open window, letting in enough light for Serge to see his lover's sheepish face.

"Nature calls," the elf said with a shrug, still standing in the open door.

Serge sighed and rubbed his eyes. "I have a spell on the door," he said.

"A spell?" Zhellian asked.

"When you come back," Serge told him, "whisper the word 'starlight,' and you can get back in without waking me up."

"Starlight," the young elf repeated.

Serge smiled and said, "Good lad."

As the door closed behind the young elf, Serge rolled over and dug himself into the thick bedclothes. His arms and legs felt heavy, and his head ached from the bottle of fine neogi rum he'd shared earlier in the evening with Zhellian. He took a deep breath and emptied his mind. Within a minute, he could feel himself drifting to sleep—

—and the alarm spell roused him again. The nettling feeling of the triggered spell made his head hurt all the more, and he sighed in frustration.

"Zhellian," he said as he rolled over and sat up in bed, "I told you to say—"

But it wasn't Zhellian.

Standing at the foot of the bed was a huge, looming shadow of deepest black. The thing was vaguely the shape of a man, but its head nearly touched the ceiling—almost eleven feet tall.

Without thinking, Serge reached out for the ring that sat on the polished wood of the nightstand next to him. He didn't so much pick up the ring as let it slide onto his finger in a fluid motion. Keeping one eye on the ring and the other on the looming shadow, Serge saw the thing move. It was leveling something at him—a crossbow? But there was no bow.

Serge did not wait to find out the hard way what was being pointed in his direction in the dead of night. He jumped up out of the bed, his tired legs all but creaking under the strain. Endless hours of physical training held him in good stead for a second—Zhellian might say third—time that night, and he was on the ceiling.

Just as his fingers touched the plaster, a blinding light filled the room. Even through his closed eyelids, Serge could make out the blazing line of a beam of light—magical light if Serge knew anything of sorcery. There was a sort of thump, like something heavy but soft hitting the floor after a long fall.

Though the last thing Serge wanted was to leap, naked, from the window of the Thrush and the Jay in the middle of the night, he made up his mind in the space of half a heartbeat that it was the only course of action open to him. He didn't know what it was he faced, but he was smart enough to know he didn't want to face it anymore.

The magic of the spider climb ring had saved him from the first attack but it would be his own legs that saved him from the second. Scrabbling on the ceiling, Serge faced the window, coiled his legs under him, and launched himself into the air. The arc would take him through the open window. He was sure he was home free when the light flashed again.

It was as if a great, invisible hand reached up from the ground, stopped him in midair, and pulled him to the floor.

The young man opened his mouth to draw in a breath but nothing came in. His body tensed, his muscles all contracted at the same time. He felt one of his ribs snap like a twig under the force of his own abdominal muscles squeezing him. He couldn't see; his vision was a mass of whirling purple and blood-red. He felt his heart stop beating all at once, and pain the likes of which he'd never imagined blazed through his chest, along his arms, into his groin, and down his legs. His bones cracked and snapped, twisted apart by his own muscles.

Serge wanted to scream, or cry, or do anything, but he couldn't. All he could do was wait in silent agony for the few moments that his reeling mind needed to realize that the rest of his body was already dead.

6

Vargussel smoothed the brilliant white gippon over his waist and studied his reflection in the full-length mirror. The padded undergarment stretched tightly across his chest. Vargussel was pleased with the way his body had held up over his fifty long, often difficult years.

He was further pleased to be back in his home. Most of the sprawling house had been closed off for years but Vargussel's suite of rooms was more than large enough to accommodate him, his wardrobe, and his library. Though the abandoned slaughterhouse served as his laboratory and shrine, he seldom stayed there for more than a few hours at a time. Accustomed as he was to the stench, even Vargussel had his limits.

Dragging his fingers through his thick, gray hair, Vargussel smiled at the thought of the previous night's success. The name of yet another of his competitors for the hand of fair Maelani had been crossed off the list, and the shield guardian had returned undetected.

Vargussel silently thanked Vecna once again not only for his continuing successes against the would-be suitors but for the labyrinth of catacombs, sewers, and forgotten dungeons that riddled the ground under New Koratia. He'd spent a good six months studying them, and even then mapped only a fraction of the tunnels—enough for the shield guardian to move in secret.

He stepped into a pair of breeches. They were made of the same green linen he preferred for most of his wardrobe and fell just to his ankles. As clean and well pressed as the gippon, the breeches made Vargussel momentarily aware of the efforts of what remained of his household staff.

With each dead relative, each married-off female cousin, a room, then a hall, then a wing of the house had been closed off. The servants were dismissed accordingly. Thousands of gold pieces worth of furniture, art, and abandoned possessions lay silently waiting under dusty sheets for someone to breathe life back into the comatose house. To Vargussel, the lonely, quiet expanse of his boyhood home had become a constant reminder of his family's abject failure.

The coffers still brimmed with gold, and the bulk of its holdings were still intact, but the family itself had not managed to survive. Was it Vargussel's fault? Perhaps. At least some of it was. After all, at fifty, he still had never married, had not produced an heir.

He buttoned the breeches to the bottom of the gippon and smoothed the fabric again.

He had been occupied, he told himself for perhaps the thousandth time. He hadn't wasted his youth. Vargussel was among the most powerful wizards in the city—in all the duchy. The fools in their floating tower were useless academics. Vargussel alone held the ear of the duke. Koratia had never had a Ducal Wizard and didn't even recognize the post, but if it did, that wizard would be Vargussel. He had, after all, built the shield guardian. That was no small task for a team of wizards, let alone to do so alone and in secret.

He slipped a bliaut off a hanger and drew it over his head. The ankle-length overgown wasn't as functional as the enchanted robe he otherwise wore almost exclusively. In the bliaut he would find no hidden pockets yielding just what he wanted when he slipped his fingers in, but for this excursion he was more concerned with impressing Maelani than with quick access to spell components. The gown, with its wine-red appliques of spiny vines, would certainly catch the young lady's eye. There were spells enough in his repertoire that needed no hand-held focus or consumable element, and the wizard had studied accordingly that morning.

When the noon hour arrived, he would go as bidden to the duke's palace. It was Vargussel's magic that elicited the duke's summons. Vargussel didn't doubt that news of the latest unfortunate death of another of New Koratia's favored sons had reached the palace, and the duke was bringing in his closest advisors to set them loose upon the murderer. Vargussel was well practiced in deceiving the duke.

He sat on a cushioned bench and slipped his feet into a pair of gaudy but fashionable pigaches. The long, upturned, pointed shoes were of a matching set with the bliaut. Vargussel admired them at the same time they made him feel a bit ridiculous. Here was but one more of the sacrifices he made to secure his family's future.

Still sitting, Vargussel closed his eyes, bowed his head, and pressed his hands gently against his chest.

"Great Vecna," he whispered, "Master of All that is Secret and Hidden, hear my prayer. Accept my sacrifices of souls and horror, accept my allegiance and my humility. Mask me from the eyes of my enemy. Hold the truth of my heart from the heart of my intended. Give me the hand of Maelani, in exchange for her father's lands, the duke's influence, and the soul of Koratia."

Vargussel sat in quiet meditation for the space of twenty-seven heartbeats, as was prescribed in the scriptures. On the twenty-eighth heartbeat, he opened his eyes, took a deep breath, and stood.

Vecna would protect him, or not. Hear him, or not. All Vargussel could do was pray, and serve, and work. As the Eighty-third Commandment taught, "Vecna helps those who help Vecna."

Vargussel stood, smoothed his clothes once more, and gave himself a last, long look in the mirror. He hated having to fuss over his appearance but it was a part of his plan, and his plan would continue apace regardless of the obstacles that might appear in his path.

He crossed to his dressing table and waved his right hand over a wooden box. His fingertips tingled, letting him know that the spell was a success. He opened the box without setting off the trap, then waved his hand over the jumble of gold and silver jewelry that filled it. His fingertips tingled once more, and he reached in with a finger to slide open the box's false bottom. From within he chose a simple band of brushed platinum. He slipped the ring on his finger, and the air around him vibrated momentarily with the item's protective magic.

Next, he drew out the dog-face amulet. Taking a moment to admire the cut of the rubies that made up its eyes, he slipped the amulet over his neck and concentrated. The link with the shield guardian rose into his consciousness. He could feel the construct standing in the gloom of the abandoned slaughterhouse, waiting for his command.

For the moment, Vargussel let the guardian sleep, if that was what its present state could be called. He closed the false bottom of the box, then its lid, resetting the enchanted triggers both times.

The wizard didn't pause for another look in the mirror but hurried out to the waiting coach for the short ride north along the wide avenue between his mansion and the palace—the palace that would soon be his.

When Regdar was shown into the duke's private office, he quickly bowed and fixed his eyes on the floor in an effort to avoid eye contact with Maelani.

He'd been summoned to the palace for a second day in a row, having to leave a steaming Naull behind at the Thrush and the Jay once more, and the duke's beautiful daughter was the last person he wanted to see. Someone had been murdered during the night in a room only a few doors from the one he shared with Naull, and the crime had drawn the attention of the duke. Though both Regdar and Naull answered the few brief questions the watch officers posed them early that morning, neither had much to report. When the duke sent for him again, Regdar drew the simple conclusion that his proximity to the scene of the crime had something to do with it.

"Ah, Regdar," the duke said, "you remember my daughter, of course."

Regdar worked to affect a polite smile, and he nodded at Maelani.

"Indeed," he answered, "My Lady. . . ."

Maelani grinned, her face alighting with a girlish pleasure that embarrassed Regdar as much as it attracted him. He forced his attention to the duke.

"Please," the duke said, "sit."

He indicated a massive, leather armchair and Regdar dutifully sat. The duke put his elbows on the broad desk in front of him and leaned forward to face Regdar. Lady Maelani seemed to float down into the chair next to Regdar. Her thin frame looked all the more delicate surrounded by the huge chair, which was a twin to Regdar's. The duke's private office was a small room, by ducal palace standards, but no less ornate it its woodwork and decorations. The martial theme—weapons, shields, and the mounted head of an owlbear—was both more pleasing to and comfortable for Regdar.

"We have a matter of some importance to discuss," the duke said, "but my daughter has appealed to me to meet you again. I indulge my only child, as I'm sure you've heard."

The duke smiled and Regdar found himself caught between nodding and shaking his head.

"I indulge my father as well," Maelani said. "I daresay we both got what we wanted today. It was especially heartening for me to hear that you will be granted a title. After all, your service to my father has guaranteed that we will all live under his protection for many good years."

Regdar nodded to the girl, but was confused. Title?

"The Lady Maelani gets ahead of herself," the duke said, with no little irritation evident in his voice. "More importantly, she gets ahead of me."

Maelani only smiled at the duke's stern countenance and said, "By moving sometimes quickly, sometimes slowly, the duke makes it difficult not to sometimes pass him, or lag too far behind."

The two nobles shared a knowing stare, making Regdar feel like he should excuse himself.

The duke finally turned to Regdar and said, "Be that as it may, in light of recent events it is not only my pleasure but my duty to grant you the title of Lord Constable of New Koratia. You will assume this post immediately."

Regdar opened his mouth to speak, but the words stuck in his throat.

Maelani leaned toward him so that their faces were only a foot apart. Looking into his eyes in a way that made Regdar even less comfortable, she said, "Welcome to the club, Lord Constable."

"Thank you," Regdar said. He knew it would take a while before he could sort out his thoughts enough to feel appropriately honored, but he added, "I serve at the will of the duke."

This elicited a girlish giggle from Maelani, who stood in a swirl of fine silk and finer jewelry. Regdar hastened to his feet, as was customary, but the duke remained seated.

"I was told," the girl said, "that I would have to leave you both once that announcement was made. I hope that whatever mysterious business you strong men have will not keep you too long."

Regdar bowed again, and Maelani swept from the room, leaving a pleasing draft of perfume in her wake. Regdar allowed himself a relieved sigh, and sat.

"As you know," the duke began without preamble, "another murder has been committed."

"Another?" Regdar asked.

The duke sighed and said, "The fifth in less than two weeks. All five of the victims died the same way, and all are of similar age and similar station."

"I know about the murder last night, but I heard of no other," Regdar said.

"We didn't realize they were murders at the time," the duke replied. "Now, well ... some things are best left to the proper circles."

Regdar nodded and said, "I take it the victims were important people."

"They would have been," the duke replied, "eventually. All five of them were still young, all were heirs to sizable family fortunes. All five came from some of the finest families in the duchy."

"I assume, Your Highness," Regdar said, "that you have named me Lord Constable and informed me of these crimes so that I can bring the murderer to justice."

The duke smiled. "Well said, Lord Constable."

"With all due respect, Your Highness," Regdar replied, "surely there must be someone more qualified than I to assume this post. I am a commoner by birth and a soldier by profession. There must be officers, trained men from the watch, who've spent a lifetime working toward that post."

"Indeed there are," the duke said. "The problem is that all of those men, and there are a few, are sons of the aristocracy. They're more politicians than soldiers, more merchants than guardsmen. They also know every one of the victims, as all of the victims knew each other."

"But that means—"

"That someone is killing the sons of the aristocracy," the duke finished for him, "and I suspect the murderer is likely a noble himself. I need someone I can trust, Regdar, and I trust you. I need someone who will not be on this murderer's list of victims. I need your common blood as much as your soldier's training."

"But the title . . ."

"The title will permit you to command the guard," the duke said. "You will have men and resources at your disposal, but you will remain outside the political circles, at least for now."

Regdar took a deep breath and nodded.

"The man who was killed at the Thrush and the Jay," he said. "I was questioned by the guards, but no one would say how he died."

"Heartstop," the duke answered. "At least, that was the determination of the Temple of Pelor."

"Heartstop?" Regdar asked. "How was it determined that it was murder then?"

"The young victim," the duke answered, "Serge d'Allion, was only twenty years old."

"Twenty?"

"Yet he died of an affliction more appropriate to a man of my own advanced years," the duke said. "The other young men—the oldest only twenty-three, the youngest a mere eighteen—died the same way. And it isn't merely that. My examiners tell me that the convulsion began in the heart but quickly coursed through them so rapidly, and with such force, that it broke every bone in their bodies. That, with no outward sign of violence."

"And the priests?" Regdar asked. "Was no effort made to return them to life?"

"Indeed," he duke replied, "in all cases. The families paid a pretty penny, called in favors, but the priests were stymied. Something not only killed these young men but sent them to oblivion, never to return."

Regdar sighed, contemplating that dark, empty, infinite fate.

"Why these five?" Regdar asked.

The duke shrugged and said, "That's something our new Lord Constable needs to find out."

"They all knew each other?"

"I have to assume so," the duke said. "This is a big city, but the noble class is small and something of a closed community. They all went to the same balls, the same weddings, the same funerals."

"To kill is easy," Regdar said, "but to kill without leaving a connection so that even a god's power could bring body and soul together again . . . that's hard."

"Again," the duke replied, "I couldn't agree more. Whoever is committing these crimes is taking great pains to make them stick and expending no little magical power in the process."

"These five families," Regdar asked, "were they allied with each other?"

"No," the duke replied, "and that only makes it more difficult to understand. Some of them were bitter rivals. Still, in the circles these families move in, alliances and animosities blow like the wind. At some point they all find themselves competing over the same resources—the same land, skilled artisans, or bits of magic and treasure."

"Then why not kill the fathers?" Regdar asked. "If it's business, why not kill the businessmen?"

"A good question," the duke said with a shrug. "Precisely the sort I'd expect the Lord Constable to ask."

Regdar nodded and considered his position. A commoner, a soldier loyal to the duke but with hardly two gold coins to rub together, and he was going to investigate the murders of young men who might have been killed over age-old family grievances or fleeting matters of commerce. He would have to question men who could buy and sell him a thousand times over and be accountable to the same men for the lives of their sons. All the while he'd be commanding men he'd never met over officers whom he'd just leapfrogged into a position of authority he never sought.

He needed to learn to stay away from the city.

Maelani stopped in the short hall that connected her father's office with the anteroom and gathered herself. She sighed and made a show of waving fresh air onto her flushed face. Maelani knew that a contingent of guards was watching her every move from concealed murder holes in the walls and ceiling. They would be some of her father's most trusted men, but even they weren't above a bit of court gossip. She had no doubt that they would take the locations of the spyholes to their graves under even the most baroque of tortures, but what would it matter that the duke's daughter was all flustered at the sight of the new lord constable?

Let them talk, Maelani thought. I've made my choice and the sooner the city gossips talk themselves through it, the better.

Not wanting to lay it on too thick, she stepped briskly down the hall.

The door to the anteroom swung open for her, and before she bothered to scan the room, she said, "Theria, don't dawdle."

Her maid rustled about in her chair, her servant's gown all wrinkled though her large frame was fairly packed into it like a sausage in its casing. The gown they had traded the day before had been specially made so that it would accommodate both Maelani and her maid. The servant's day-to-day uniform enjoyed a much less expert tailoring. The maid stood, glancing quickly back and forth between Maelani and the man she'd been sitting next to.

"Vargussel," Maelani said, the moment she remembered the man's name.

Vargussel stood while bending at the waist in a sort of ascending bow. His thin lips twisted into a grin Maelani had seen on a hundred faces, though they were always much younger faces. A man of Vargussel's age shouldn't look at a woman her age with a grin like that.

Theria stepped away from the older man, her own face puckered in a most unattractive way.

"Oh, Mistress," the maid said as she swished up next to her employer. "I understand you know this ... gentleman?"

Vargussel nodded like some kind of carrion bird inspecting a carcass and said, "It has been my distinct pleasure to make the lady's acquaintance on a number of occasions. Lady Maelani ..."

Maelani sighed and said, "Ah, yes, Vargussel. How do you do?"

"Well," the man simpered, his face turning a blotchy red. "And My Lady?"

"I am fine, thank you," Maelani replied, making it a point to be nothing more than curtly polite. "So, Theria," she continued, turning to her maid, "let us—"

Vargussel stepped forward, not exactly blocking Maelani's path, but both women were startled by his sudden approach. Theria yelped and put a hand to her chest. Vargussel hurriedly stepped back, blushing and sweating. It all made for a scene Maelani would replay in her most humiliating nightmares.

A waft of some heavy, damp stench slid across her as if the air itself had suddenly become greasy, and it was all Maelani could do to keep her face from registering her revulsion. The smell had come from Vargussel.

Theria, on the other hand, made no attempt to disguise the fact that the room contained something rotten.

"Goodness, sir," she said, looking away and pressing her chubby fingers to her mouth and nose.

"My apologies," Vargussel said, hunching into another bow. "My . . . experiments . . . in the service of the duke . . ."

Maelani watched him stammer and hedge with no interest at all. She took one step closer to the door, feeling Theria move to join her, when Vargussel put up a hand.

"Please, Lady Maelani," he said.

The duke's daughter stopped, pursed her lips, and waited for the man to speak.

"Lady . . ." Vargussel began, then he wrung his hands.

"Vargussel," she said, "please do not let me keep you. I'm certain your business with my father is of the utmost urgency."

"They'll send for me," he said, "when the duke is ready for me. In the meantime, though, if I might have just the briefest morsel of your time."

Maelani set her weight all on her right foot and crossed her arms in front of her chest.

"I, uh . . ." Vargussel began.

Theria put a hand on Maelani's arm and the duke's daughter looked down at her maid. The woman's beady eyes darted between Maelani and the door, her face a caricature of impatience. Maelani lifted an eyebrow to put her off, but said nothing.

Vargussel cleared his throat, and Maelani made a show of granting him her attention. The man seemed to have calmed himself.

"My family," he said, "was once one of the duchy's most prominent. We continue to control substantial resources, as the lady is certainly aware. The finest of the duchy's bloodlines mingles with my own, and it has been my honor to serve the duke in matters arcane and mundane alike. I have property and position, and I am unmarried."

Maelani's blood ran cold.

"Your father," the wretched man continued, "has made it clear that a marriage is in the offing. I beg . . ."

Vargussel finally looked her in the eyes, and if Maelani's blood could have run any colder, it would have. His eyes were hard, almost lifeless, but possessed of a keen intelligence that made Maelani almost as afraid as she was surprised.

"No," he corrected himself. "I do not beg, my lady, because I do not need to. I have the position, the blood, the service, and the will to make you my wife."

Maelani drew a slow breath, doing her best to ignore the man's odor, and said, "Sir, you assume much."

"I do," Vargussel answered. "I am a blunt man. That I admit freely. I have spent my life in serious study, in the consideration of matters of extraordinary significance and ancient power, but I have always put the needs of the duchy before my own and before the needs of my family. Now it is my family and yours both in need of an heir. You will find no better match—not among the sniveling brats of this city's bourgeoisie."

"Won't I?" Maelani asked.

"Sir," Theria cut in, "please accept my apologies, but I fear you are making the lady uncomfortable."

Maelani regarded her maid with a smile. Good old Theria: scared all the time, but dependable in a pinch.

Vargussel turned his gaze on Theria, who withered from it and stepped behind her mistress.

"Still," Maelani said to Vargussel, "you assume much."

Vargussel smiled and bowed his head slightly. Maelani took stock of the man again. He was taller than her and not badly put together. She thought that he might even have been attractive one day, decades past. His clothing was of the finest cut, but easily eight months or more out of date. She couldn't help but look at his shoes, though she preferred to at least try to stare the presumptuous man down.

"I have more to offer," he said, "than merely my family's fortune and loyalty. I will beg My Lady's forgiveness for one more transgression of protocol."

Maelani opened her mouth to withdraw that forgiveness, but Vargussel spoke over her.

"I love you," he said.

Theria gasped again, and Maelani could feel the maid peeking out from behind her.

"I—" Maelani started.

"Sir!" Theria all but yelped.

Without a glance at the maid, Vargussel said, "I love you, My Lady, in a most chaste and sincere way. I have known you all your life and have watched you grow from a troublesome child to a young woman of such grace and beauty, a mere duchy is not enough for you. Make me your husband, Maelani, and I'm certain you will grow to love me as I love you. Make me your duke, Maelani, and I will make you a queen."

Maelani realized she still had her mouth open, and she closed it, tapping her teeth together. She ignored the feeling of Theria's eyes burning into the back of her neck, and she worked hard on what she would say next. Vargussel stared at her, his hands pressed together as if he was praying. He was two strides away from her and she could still smell him.

"Vargussel," she said, "I know that you have served my father and the Duchy of Koratia well on many occasions for many years, so I will honor that and not repeat your hasty words to the duke. I will simply remind you, sir, that it is inappropriate for anyone to—"

"I know," Vargussel interrupted, drawing a raised eyebrow from Maelani. "I know all that. I know everything you're going to say, but all I can do is lay myself bare before you, My Lady, and await our life together."

"You smell," Maelani said, her mouth running far ahead of her mind, which sat by cheering.

"Lady . . . ?" Vargussel started, his face turning blotchy red again.

"You smell," Maelani said, more loudly. "You reek of a sewer, you hideous, dried up old prune."

"Lady, I—"

"Will shut your stinking hole and let me finish, you wretch," the young woman continued.

Theria giggled and Vargussel flashed the maid a horrified glance.

"You think I could love you?" Maelani continued. "How could you think that? Is that what drives you in your most arcane and mysterious studies in your filth-reeking laboratory, you gutter rat? Is it those grimy, little fantasies that fuel your twisted old mind when you shop for last year's ridiculous pigaches? Look at you. Look at yourself."

Vargussel clamped his mouth shut, his lips pressing into a white line.

"Mistress," Theria whispered, tugging on her arm.

Maelani jerked her arm out of her maid's grip and held up a thin finger at Vargussel.

The door opened and a guard stepped in. The noise startled all three of the anteroom's occupants and they shuffled uncomfortably, taking stock of themselves before the intruder.

"Vargussel," the guard said, looking from the old wizard to the duke's daughter to the maid.

Maelani could see the man trying to work out the situation and had to assume he hadn't heard the conversation. She turned to the guard, who bowed, then she strode quickly to the outer door. Theria hustled behind her, shooting Vargussel one last look of stern disapproval.

"Sir," the guard said, "the duke will see you now."

Maelani let Theria close the door behind them without looking back.

Vargussel felt as if his blood had frozen solid. His veins and arteries were like a second skeleton, propping him up for all to see in his perfect, crystalline humiliation. He felt as if, at the slightest touch, he would shatter into a million shards of stupidity, ignorance, and self-loathing, and that every one of those million shards would be coated in the greasy stench of an abandoned slaughterhouse, his new family home, the final resting place of the tiny shred of human dignity that remained to his miserable—

"Are you all right, sir?" a voice asked, sending a shiver up Vargussel's back.

The wizard blinked, shook his head, and his eyes fell on the face of the guard. Where he was, what he was doing, and more than that who he was, flooded back into Vargussel. His blood flowed once more, his mind raced anew, and his skin tingled with anticipation.

"I am fine," he said, smiling at the sound of his own voice. The words came out steadily, in a tone deep and strong.

The guard nodded and gestured to the door.

"The duke awaits," he said.

Vargussel grinned at the man and said, "Indeed he does, son."

The duke awaits, Vargussel thought. The Duke of Koratia, one of the most powerful men in world, awaits me. He cannot function without me. The city, the duchy, the world itself would crumble without me. I am the man the duke needs most, and it will be the duke who convinces his daughter that—

"Sir?" the guard said, again breaking into Vargussel's reverie.

The wizard took a deep breath, nodded, and followed the guard through the door.

As they passed through the short hall to the duke's private office, Vargussel adjusted his clothing, shook his shoulders, and finished gathering his wits about him. When the guard opened the door to the office Vargussel was fully himself again, prepared to once more make himself indispensable to his duke.

"Vargussel," the duke said," there you are, old man."

Once, Vargussel would have been delighted to hear the duke refer to him as "old man." For a man like the duke, that was a sign of acceptance. After his utter failure with Maelani, however, the greeting made Vargussel feel like . . . an old man.

"Are you all right?" the duke asked.

Vargussel cleared his throat, found his mouth as dry as dust, and croaked out, "Certainly, Your Highness."

"You look like a cavalryman who forgot his codpiece," the duke joked. "Come in."

Vargussel shuffled into the office in his ridiculous shoes, and just then became aware of the thin sheen of sweat that coated his entire body. He looked up at the duke and forced a smile. The duke looked back at him with narrowed eyes, sincere concern on his face.

"Your Highness," Vargussel said, "sent for me?"

The duke nodded and motioned to a chair. Vargussel, knees shaking, all but staggered to a seat—then jumped when someone touched his back and said, "Excuse me, sir."

Vargussel turned and realized he'd almost sat in another man's lap. The duke was chuckling and the man, who Vargussel didn't recognize, looked embarrassed. Vargussel shuffled to the other chair, made a conscious effort to see that it was empty, and sat. One of his knees cracked painlessly but loudly on the way down. Vargussel closed his eyes and sighed.

His eyes still closed, Vargussel heard the duke snap his fingers and there were hurried footsteps, the sound of water being poured into a glass, and the guard's voice again, saying, "Sir?"

Vargussel opened his eyes, took the glass of water from the guard, and drank it down with shaking hands in one, unsatisfying gulp.

"Thank you," he said to neither the guard nor the duke in particular.

The guard took the glass and left the room in an embarrassed hurry.

"Vargussel?" the duke said, his voice heavy with concern.

Vargussel breathed deeply and looked at the duke, who was sitting behind his impressive desk, eyeing him.

"Your Highness," Vargussel said, "please accept my most sincere apologies. My experiments are reaching a critical phase, and I have to admit that lost sleep has been the price of my success in the laboratory. I hope you will forgive my state, as I hope you will believe that I am as able as I am willing to serve the duchy in whatever manner Your Highness desires."

"Good," the duke replied, glancing at the other man. "For a moment I thought something had happened in the anteroom. I trust you saw Lady Maelani on her way out."

Vargussel felt the blood drain from his face, but he said, "Yes, Your Highness."

"And you're certain all is well?"

"I am, Your Highness," Vargussel replied, "most assuredly."

"Very well," said the duke, sitting back in his chair and motioning to the strange man. "This is Regdar, who just moments ago accepted the position of Lord Constable of New Koratia. Lord Constable, may I introduce Vargussel, a most capable wizard and a loyal friend to the duchy."

Regdar tipped his head at Vargussel and said, "Vargussel. It is my pleasure."

"Lord Constable?" Vargussel said.

"Yes," replied the duke. "Regdar is one of my most trusted soldiers, and he has agreed to serve the duchy in the investigation of these murders."

Vargussel swallowed, his mouth and throat still dry. He dabbed the sweat from his brow with his fingertips, which served only to send the perspiration dripping into his eyes.

Blinking madly, he said, "He has? I mean . . . has he indeed?"

"Are you quite certain you're not ill, old man?" asked the duke.

"I am, Your Highness," Vargussel replied. He shifted in his seat to sit up straighter and he turned to face the new lord constable. "My apologies, Lord Constable. Please feel free to assume that, unless his highness should say otherwise, my services are at your disposal, such as they may be."

"Precisely what I hoped to hear," the duke said.

Regdar said, "Thank you, Vargussel."

"Yes," the old wizard said, putting his hands on the arms of the chair to signal that he was intending to stand, "well, there we are."

The duke put out a hand and the wizard sat back, clenching his teeth so they wouldn't chatter.

"Easy there, Vargussel," the duke said. "Why don't we sit a moment and let you rest. If you're to be of any help to the lord constable, to me, or to anyone—including yourself—you should rest, and perhaps eat."

"I will," Vargussel replied, "thank you, sir."

Well, the old wizard thought, he feels sorry for me. I am a pitiful old man.

He cleared his throat again and once more sat up straight. He turned his attention to Regdar and looked the man up and down. He was huge, a behemoth.

A soldier, indeed.

Vargussel smiled as he took stock of the man's too-small head, and he made up his mind all at once that the new Lord Constable would be as easy to manipulate as the duke and as unlikely to appear at Vargussel's door.

"Lord Constable," Vargussel said, "were you acquainted with any of the young victims?"

"No," Regdar replied.

Vargussel waited patiently for more, but soon realized that the new lord constable had finished speaking with that one word.

"Have you a plan, then," the wizard asked, "for your investigation? A strategy for driving this madman—whoever he may be—to the cold light of the duke's justice?"

Regdar glanced at the duke, then said, "No."

Vargussel opened his mouth to speak, but before he could, Regdar added, "Not yet."

"Not yet, indeed," the wizard replied. "Well, all in due time, I'm sure."

"Regdar has only held the post for five minutes, Vargussel," the duke said. "I'm sure he'll make us all proud."

"You were born a common man, then?" Vargussel asked Regdar, not intentionally ignoring the duke. "Not from the aristocracy, are you?"

"No," Regdar replied.

"A common foot soldier, then?" Vargussel pressed. "A man with arms like maces, tempered in the blood of the enemies of the duchy, is that it?"

"Vargussel . . ." the duke started to say.

"I suppose so," Regdar replied.

"Good for you," the wizard said. "I'm certain your family has never been more thrilled."

"I have no family," Regdar replied.

"Not yet," added the duke—all too quickly for Vargussel's tastes.

"Well . . . I . . . uh . . ." Regdar stammered.

"Oh, he'll have a family all right," the duke said.

"A young lady, is there, Lord Constable?" Vargussel teased.

"Actually . . ." the lord constable started, but it was the duke who finished for him.

"Let's just say that my daughter has a way of getting what she wants."

Vargussel's heart seemed to stop in his chest. Tingling fingers of cold death worried about his shoulders and spine. His legs trembled, and sweat broke out on his forearms.

"Your daughter?" he managed to say.

The duke chuckled and winked at him, and Vargussel found it difficult to breathe.

"Yes ... well ..." Vargussel said. "Yes ... why not?"

"Why not indeed," said the duke.

Because I'm going to kill him, Vargussel said only to himself. *Because my shield guardian will hold a rod to his head that will blast his soul into shreds. Because he is now on my list. Because she will not have what she wants, but what she needs. Because ...*

"Yes," he said aloud, "why not indeed, Your Highness ... Lord Constable ... why not, indeed."

Naull found it difficult to keep up with Regdar and the tall, skinny man who owned the Thrush and the Jay. The skinny man was walking faster than most people ran. If Naull could spare the energy to look at him, she fully expected Regdar to be sweating and panting from the exertion. He'd insisted on wearing his heavy, cumbersome armor and he clanked his way up the stairs like a steel golem.

She wanted to be angry with him, but she was also smart enough to identify jealousy, even in herself. So he was the Lord Constable—so what? It meant nothing, except that he was a member of the aristocracy and would never be able to marry her, though he could marry the duke's daughter. That would make him the duke, eventually, and Naull one of his subjects.

To Carceri with it, she thought. I am jealous.

When the tall, skinny man stopped at one of the wide double doors in the hall at the top of the stairs, Naull wiped the sweat from her forehead with the back of her hand and took a deep breath.

"Please tell me this is it," she said, making a show of shaking her tired legs.

Regdar smiled at her in that endearing way he had. She suppressed the urge to slap his face and instead turned her attention to the inn's owner.

"Yes, madam," he said, "this is the . . . unfortunate room."

Naull ignored the sarcastic tone she was sure she heard in his use of the word "madam," and she waited patiently for him to finish unlocking the doors.

"Leave us here," Regdar told the proprietor. "We'll come find you when we're finished."

The tall, skinny man raised one tall, skinny eyebrow and looked down his tall, skinny nose judgmentally at Regdar. He swung the doors open and stepped out of the way, clicked his heels on the marble floor, and tipped his head in a cursory bow.

Regdar walked into the room and Naull followed, but not before she smiled graciously at the man and said, "Thank you, sir. Do let us know if any more murders occur while we're here."

The man's face blanched and Naull closed the doors behind her.

The room was as opulent as the one Naull shared with Regdar. The massive bed was draped in the finest silk and wool, and the marble floor was covered with exotic rugs that might have been woven by elves. The furniture was quite old but in impeccable repair. The air smelled of lavender from the scented candles burning in gold sconces. Lingering just at the edge of Naull's senses, though, was another scent. It was the odor of something burned, the scent of a lightning-struck tree . . . something like that.

Regdar strode purposefully to a small table set for two. On the duke's orders, the body had been taken away but nothing else had been touched. The remains of a light supper from the night before was congealing on plates of the finest porcelain, and the dregs of a bottle of vintage elven dew wine stained a pair of crystal glasses.

"Our friend had a guest?" Naull asked.

Regdar nodded and said, "A young elf he was . . . seeing, I guess. The duke asked me not to be too specific about that in public. I guess it would cause some kind of scandal."

"Why?" Naull asked. "The sons of the rich and famous aren't supposed to date elves?"

Regdar actually blushed and looked down, pretending to examine the fine linen tablecloth.

"What?" Naull asked.

Regdar cleared his throat and said, "In the army, it's more common than you . . . well, anyway . . . we're not supposed to ask . . ."

When Naull realized what he was saying, she nodded vigorously and felt her cheeks flush.

"I get it," she said. "Well, that's hardly a crime—wouldn't draw a death sentence anyway. Are the rich and famous of New Koratia so uptight that they'd kill one of their prodigal sons just for dallying with other prodigal sons?"

"I wouldn't know," Regdar said. "I don't think so, but we shouldn't discount it as a possibility. These people are very sensitive when it comes to children, bloodlines, and all that."

"Really?" Naull asked, crossing her arms over her chest. "Do tell me more, Lord Constable. Your own bloodline, for instance. Is it clear of all such impropriety?"

Regdar looked at her with narrowed eyes, seemed to think about it for a second, then sighed and said, "That's not fair, Naull."

"Well," Naull replied, "If you say so, milord."

"You don't have to call me that."

"Don't I?" she asked. "What shall I call you, Lord Constable?"

Regdar sighed and turned away. Naull felt suddenly very petty and just as suddenly cold and unsafe.

"Could the food have been poisoned?" she asked, in an effort to rescue them both.

Regdar seemed as relieved as she was to move on to the business at hand.

"Perhaps," he replied. He gestured to the table and stepped back.

Naull brought to mind the simple cantrip she'd prepared that morning on Regdar's request. It required no material components or focuses, so all she did was murmur the proper incantation and move the fingers of her right hand just so.

She let her gaze fall over the table. When her eyelids started to twitch, she knew the magic was active, but nothing about the cold food and warm wine looked different. If anything in the general vicinity of the tabletop had been poisoned, she would have seen it glow a subtle purple. There was no such glow.

"No," she said to Regdar. "Nothing's poisoned. At least, not the food or wine."

Regdar nodded and looked around the room.

"There's only one way in or out," he said, "besides the windows anyway."

"None of the other guests saw or heard anything?" Naull asked.

"Nothing of value," Regdar said. "Some reported sounds of a ruckus, of heavy footsteps in the hall."

"So someone heavy came in the front door and ... did what?" Naull asked.

Regdar shrugged.

"Aren't there guards in here?" she asked. "I've seen guards."

Moving in and out of the Thrush and the Jay over the past several days, Naull had even commented to Regdar on the professional, experienced mien of the inn's uniformed guards. She'd even surreptitiously cast a spell that showed her the auras of their enchanted weapons and armor. No expense had been spared.

"The guards are kept outside," Regdar said, "and in the common areas on the ground floor. Apparently, the guests' privacy takes precedence here. There are no guards roaming the halls."

Naull sighed and said, "No loose lips to wag about midnight indiscretions, youthful or otherwise. Unfortunately, no loose lips to wag about murderers either."

"I guess so," Regdar replied. "The entrances are so well guarded, though, the question isn't so much how did our man get into this room but rather, how did he get into the Thrush and the Jay in the first place?"

"I prepared a spell that might answer that question," Naull said. "It would be easy enough to discern if there's some secret way in or out of this room, but it would take a while to cover the rest of the inn."

Regdar nodded and said, "Go ahead."

Naull called the spell to mind. This one was just a bit more difficult than the last, requiring a very peculiar cadence to the incantation and an overly precise dip of the left ring finger. She performed the spell adequately, though, and was reassured by a smaller, nettling feeling in her eyes. She scanned the room, concentrating on the uncomfortable sensation.

Regdar was smart enough not to disturb her, even after she'd made a full circuit of the room without giving her report. She concentrated more deeply and was rewarded by a growing pull on her senses that made her turn her head to the left, and tilt down. She felt like something was gently but firmly pulling her face to the floor, through it, down, deeper. When she closed her eyes, the pull was broken.

Naull shook her head to clear the spell from her consciousness. She needed a few seconds to focus again on Regdar, who was approaching with a hand extended and a worried look on his face.

"I'm all right, Your Lordship," she said, stepping away from him.

Regdar pressed his lips together and sighed.

"There's a secret door," she said, breaking the uncomfortable moment she was happy enough to have instigated. "Not in this room, but somewhere at least a couple floors down—likely the basement or the wine cellar."

Regdar nodded and said, "Handy spell."

Naull shrugged and replied, "I have my moments."

"What else have you got up your sleeve?" he asked.

Naull looked around and her eyes settled on a cloak that was draped over one of the chairs at the table. It was a fine cloak.

"Was anything stolen?" she asked.

Regdar shook his head, then stopped to think about it.

"I don't know," he said.

Naull crossed to the chair and touched the cloak. It was made of very expensive silk and quite masterfully tailored. She patted the length of it and felt something not only swing against the chair behind it, but she also felt lumps in one of the cloak's pockets.

"Something in there?" Regdar asked.

Naull slipped the cloak off the back of the chair, and said, "I guess so."

Under the cloak, hung on the back of the chair, was a thin leather belt on which was suspended a stunning jeweled rapier and a long dagger of matching design. Even Naull recognized them as a significant pair of weapons, likely a family heirloom.

Regdar stood next to her and pulled the weapons belt from the chair. He examined the rapier closely with a soldier's eye for both form and function, then drew the dagger. The blade was so highly polished that it sent up a flash of reflected candlelight that made both Naull and Regdar blink.

"It's a safe bet these belonged to the victim," Regdar said. "That's an aristocrat's weapon if I ever saw one."

Regdar slid the dagger back into its sheath and returned the belt to the chair.

Naull turned her attention to the cloak, fishing around in the pocket instead of looking at Regdar. Her hand closed on something made of cool metal and she drew out a long, thin vial of brushed electrum, stoppered and sealed with wax. There was something else in the same pocket, and Naull reached in again, still holding the vial. She wrapped her finger around a length of soft cord and pulled out a small, suede pouch.

She set the vial and the pouch carefully on the table. The telltale sound of coins rattled in the pouch. Naull hung the cloak on another chair as Regdar examined the contents of the purse.

"Gold," he said, "and platinum."

Regdar dropped the pouch on the table and stepped back, examining the newfound riches with a creased forehead.

"If you were going to murder someone," he asked, "would you leave this kind of loot behind?"

"I'll bet you double or nothing for that pouch of coins that at least some of this stuff is magical, too," Naull said.

"Can you find out for sure?"

Naull nodded, and brought a third spell to mind. Regdar took a few steps away from the table.

"It's all right," she said. "It's not a fireball."

Regdar smiled sheepishly and gestured for her to continue.

Naull cast the spell—again, not the most complicated casting. She was rewarded immediately with the presence of magical auras sprinkled about the room.

She narrowed her gaze, kept her breathing even, and concentrated.

"The vial," she said in a distracted monotone, "the rapier, the dagger, and the cloak."

She took a deep breath and narrowed her focus again, keeping calm, waiting, and it all started becoming more clear.

"Something in the vial," she whispered, "not the vial itself. It's an enchantment, I think . . . a potion. . . ."

Her voice trailed off, then she looked up, scanning the rest of the room. Regdar's magical accoutrements glowed in her vision, as did her own—and there was something on the door.

She didn't risk stepping closer, just let her mind concentrate on the door. It was a weak aura typical of old signs.

She closed her eyes, let out a breath she hadn't realized she was holding, and let the spell fade.

"The door," Naull said. "A spell was cast on the door."

"What kind of spell?" Regdar asked.

"An abjuration," she said.

"What does that do?"

"All sorts of things," she answered. "It's a school of magic, not a specific spell. It's very weak now, and it looks like it was never very strong to begin with. I'd bet it was designed either to hold the door shut or make the caster aware of someone passing through it."

"Like an alarm?" Regdar asked.

Naull nodded.

"What about the rest of it?" he asked.

"The potion is likely meant to make you do something," she said, "or think something . . . I don't know. The cloak, the rapier, and the dagger, I have no idea. Other spells could tell me, but I would need a few days at least to get through all of them by myself."

"We should take them with us, then," Regdar said.

"The murderer wasn't interested in all this valuable magic or gold and platinum coins," Naull replied.

"Apparently not," Regdar said.

"So," said Naull, "it's personal, then."

Regdar nodded, then picked up the weapons belt, the pouch, and the vial. He nodded at the cloak and Naull picked it up, draping it over one forearm.

"Can you cast a spell," Regdar asked, "like the one that sealed the door, if that's what it did?"

"I can," she answered. "Actually, I have one in mind that'll likely do a better job of it. I'll be able to open it, but it'll be a tough one for anyone else."

"Good," Regdar said. "I think we've seen all we need to see here for now."

Regdar stepped back, gesturing for her to precede him to the door.

"So, Your Lord Constableness," she said, not moving, "is your high and lofty office going to cover the twenty-five Merchants in gold dust—twenty-five each go, mind you—that I'll need to cast the identify spells?"

Regdar rubbed his chin with his big, callused fingers.

"You know what?" he said with a twinkle in his eye. "I don't know."

Maelani slipped the fine linen camise over her naked body and luxuriated in the soft caress of the floral-perfumed fabric. She shook her long, clean hair out of the plunging neckline and reached for the stomacher of azure silk that Theria had laid out for her.

Maelani had taken longer than she'd liked to finally get rid of the ever-present maid so she could dress herself in peace. Theria wasn't a gossip, and she kept any number of secrets for Maelani, but that didn't stop her from whining or from trying to talk Maelani out of this plan, that scheme, or the other subterfuge. It was as if the chubby little maid wanted Maelani to settle for some loveless, political marriage.

Maelani wrapped the stomacher beneath her breasts, adjusting the fit to make the most of what nature had given her. She smiled at herself in the full-length silver mirror and tried to see herself as Regdar would see her.

In both of their short meetings she'd found the Lord Constable to be surprisingly nervous, but that was a reaction from men that Maelani was accustomed to. Since outgrowing her awkward years and coming into the full flower of womanhood, Maelani had become quite comfortable with the attention of the opposite sex. Beauty often made the strongest of men quiver in his boots, the most eloquent choke on the simplest greeting, and the bravest flee in abject terror.

She drew a cloth-of-gold bodice around her waist and began lacing it. Maelani hadn't done this complex task by herself for so long that she found herself fumbling with the lacing. Growing increasingly frustrated, she even had to stop and start over from the beginning, but finally she managed to get it well secured. Examining herself from both sides in the mirror, she made fine adjustments to the garment's fit, again in an effort to flatter her graceful but modest curves.

She stepped into a long skirt and drew it up. The skirt hung provocatively on her hips, revealing a scandalous hint of the trans-lucent linen camise between it and the bodice. Looking at herself in the mirror, Maelani blushed.

There were things no man could resist and if done properly, a lady could take advantage of those things and still be a lady.

Maelani silently thanked the gods that her mother had lived just long enough to give her that advice and more. Had she been raised exclusively by her father, she might have made a fine man, a capable soldier, and a valiant leader, but she would certainly have been a washout as a lady.

"True power," she whispered to her reflection, repeating words her mother had said to her a thousand times, "speaks with a wom-an's soft caress."

With a giggle, she slipped into a pair of gilded sandals enchanted to allow her to levitate. She found the experience of floating aloft unpleasant, but she had plans for the slippers that night. Next she slid a pair of cloth-of-gold gloves up her forearms. The gloves fit her to her elbows, and the fine silk only hinted at the greater softness of the flesh beneath. She kept her gloved fingers conspicuously free of rings. It was a message most men missed, but she would send it anyway. The duke would die if he knew she was leaving the palace without so much as a ring of protection, but what her father didn't know. . . .

Maelani regarded the whole outfit with a wider grin. She was beautiful. She was the sort of girl any man would fall in love with on sight.

"Potion?" she asked her reflection. "What potion?"

She slipped the vial she'd purchased from Vrilanda into one of her gloves, taking care that it wouldn't show, even as she assured herself that she wouldn't need it.

She took a deep breath and carefully picked up a shimmering, golden diadem from her dressing table. Though it was hardly the flashiest piece in the family's collection, she'd had to send Theria to the vaults with a note to get it drawn out for her. Maelani slipped it onto her forehead, letting the cool aquamarine that dangled from it slowly grow warm against her forehead. The diadem would keep the hair out of her eyes while allowing it to flow free. Men liked that, Maelani knew.

"My lords, ladies, and gentlemen," she said to the mirror, "may I present Duke Regdar and the Duchess Maelani."

For the thousandth time, Naull," Regdar said, a vein standing out on his forehead and sweat beading on his upper lip, "I have no interest in the duke's daughter."

Naull shrugged and turned away from him so he couldn't see her smile. She crossed to the bed they'd shared since returning to the city and sat down. She sank into the opulent duvet and ran her fingers through her hair. She was careful to give Regdar a good look at her long neck.

She heard him take a step toward her and her breath caught. As if sensing her reaction, he stopped.

"You like to tease me," he said.

"You like to . . ." she started, but wasn't sure what to say.

"Ah," he said. "No comeback? No witty reproach of my honor, or the duke's, or his daughter's?"

Naull clenched her teeth to keep from laughing as Regdar walked up behind her. Even out of his armor his tread was heavy and solid on the marble floor. She could feel him looming over her.

"What do you want me to say, Naull?" he asked.

She shook her head, and Regdar's fingertips brushed her hair. His touch was impossibly gentle for a man who had spent his life wielding a sword in defense of duke and duchy. She tipped her head just a fraction of an inch, leaning into him.

"This Lord Constable business is temporary," he said. "There are crimes being committed, and the duke has chosen this way to stop them. He will choose a husband for Maelani as well, in time, a man who will be his successor. He may be casting about for that man now, but soon enough the realities of the situation will become apparent. The next duke will not have been born a commoner, Naull. It will not be me."

Naull felt the heat of a tear in the corner of her eye and she took a deep breath.

"Naull?"

"It won't be you?" she asked. "Are you sure? Can you be sure? He might have made his decision."

Regdar's hand dropped away from her hair and he took a step back from her. Despite herself, she turned to look at him but saw only his strong back.

"He could give you an order," she said. "Lord Constable, or common foot soldier, could you deny him his chosen successor?"

Regdar turned and Naull was taken aback by the smile on his face. There was no doubt there, as there seldom was. In his eyes she saw the same lack of subterfuge and guile, the same simple honor and truth that made him who he was, that made him the man she loved.

"I have sworn to follow the duke's orders," he said, "even unto my own death, but. . . ."

Naull shook her head and wiped away a tear with her fingertip. She stood and stepped into his warm, strong embrace. His arms folded around her and her body felt at once weak and strong, vulnerable and safe. She breathed him in.

"What do I want you to say?" she asked, trying not to cry. "I want you to say you love me. I want you to say you will marry me. I want you to say that you'll stay with me every day for the rest of our lives."

She felt him sigh, in his chest and in the breeze of his breath against her hair. He took a breath to speak and she felt that too, then felt his body stop all at once, become rigid and alert.

It wasn't the reaction she'd hoped for. When she stepped away from him, he let her go. She looked up and saw his face turned to one side, his head cocked, his mouth open. Naull's blood went cold.

"What is it?" she whispered, instantly bringing to mind a spell.

He held up a finger to quiet her and shook his head.

He was looking at the doors to their private veranda. The floor-to-ceiling doors were divided into panes of glass, any one of which was too small for a human to climb through. Sheer draperies covered them, letting in only enough of the street lamps' light to let them know the sun had set. None of the sounds of the busy street below were audible.

"Is someone out there?" she whispered.

Naull scanned the draperies and saw no shadows behind them. Anyone on the veranda would be visible in silhouette. No one was there.

The sound of steel sliding on steel startled her and she whirled to see Regdar holding his sword, its enchanted, razor-sharp blade glowing in the room's soft light. He crossed to the windows, his steps all but silent, unlike only moments before. When he was close enough to touch the draperies, he slipped one edge an inch to the side and peered out. She could tell he saw nothing, at least not right away.

Naull heard a scuffling sound at the same time Regdar did. The fighter stepped back as he let go of the drape. When the sound came again, Naull thought it might be a shoe slipping on stone. It definitely came from outside the window. The spell she'd brought to mind was among her most potent. If necessary she could erect an enchanted wall made from nothing but the invisible wind, which would protect them both from the intruder at least long enough to determine who or what it was. She tried not to think about the damage the wind would do to their beautiful room.

Realizing that the wind wall could just as easily blow Regdar off his feet if he was in the wrong place at the wrong time, Naull padded closer to him. As she moved, and the still air of the room ruffled her silk chemise across her skin, Naull felt all the more vulnerable. She had never worn armor and was more comfortable in light attire than Regdar had become, but if she was going to fight for her life, she wanted to at least be dressed.

Regdar saw her approaching, and he held out his free hand to stop her. She touched the elbow of his sword arm. When he glanced at her she jerked her head back once and whispered, "Back up."

He narrowed his eyes at her, confused and impatient. In response, Naull wiggled her fingers and arched an eyebrow. The crude, improvised sign language registered on Regdar quickly enough and he stepped back. Just then, a shadow slid across the draperies.

The intruder appeared human enough, but the shadow's size could have been exaggerated by the light. The thing could have been the size of a halfling or a stone giant.

Naull stepped in front of Regdar and brought her hands up, twisting the fingers of her left hand into the spell's first position while her right hand reached for—

She didn't have her pouches. She didn't have the material component for the spell.

The shadow moved to the door. Naull could sense Regdar's huge sword in the ready position behind her. She turned, held one finger up to stop him, and took three fast, long strides to the nightstand.

The polished brass door handle turned slowly just as Naull's fingers found the right pouch and reached inside. There was a barely audible click as the door unlatched. Naull's hand wrapped around a feather and a miniature silk fan no longer than her little finger.

The door moved, a torturously slow quarter of an inch at a time, as Naull began casting the spell. She tried to whisper but the intruder must have heard her, or perhaps sensed the growing magic in the air of the room. The door stopped opening but made no move to close.

Warm air washed over Naull as she completed the spell, and she had to close her eyes against the blast. When she felt her chemise flip up over her face she was momentarily embarrassed, but quickly regained her wits. She stepped back, keeping one forearm over her eyes. The sound of the wind in the confined space was deafening but in a few steps she could at least see again.

The door to the veranda blew open, revealing a young woman struggling with her own wildly uncontrolled clothing. One of the glass panes shattered and the woman shrieked, ducking away and losing her footing in the gale. Regdar dashed forward, and Naull saw that he no longer held his sword. Her skin crawled with fear when she realized what would happen if he'd dropped the sword in the swirling wind. The blade would become a whirling, wind-driven, razor-sharp menace, chopping down anything unfortunate enough to cross its unpredictable path.

"Regdar!" Naull screamed into the wind wall. "No!"

He was forcing his way into the wind, bending low and pushing through the wall. Naull knew he was strong but she hadn't imagined he was that strong. He was passing through the wall of air, reaching out for the woman. The intruder was in serious danger of falling off the veranda and suffering the fifty-foot drop to the lamplit street below. Naull wasn't entirely certain why Regdar wanted to prevent that

"Regdar!" she screamed again.

Just below the roar of the wind, Naull could hear a woman scream. Regdar reached the doorframe and held on tightly, still reaching with his other hand for the woman on the veranda. He turned to Naull and shouted something that she couldn't hear. She would have read his lips, or tried to, at least, had her chemise not blown up into her face again, leaving her blind and naked from the waist down. She struggled to pull the silk away from her face but the wind and her own panic made her tug too hard. She heard something tear and felt the garment shift to one side. The material came away from her face in time for Naull to see Regdar pulling the strange woman into the room.

Naull searched her mind for a useful spell but there was little left after the examination of the crime scene. She hadn't planned her day with the expectation of fighting off intruders in what was supposed to be the most secure inn in the duchy.

Regdar and the woman fell hard onto the marble floor, and Naull's chemise blew up in her face again. She could hear Regdar shouting but couldn't understand him. She grabbed at the silk in front of her face.

"—that damn thing stop!" Regdar shouted, his voice echoing in the suddenly quiet, still air.

The wind blew itself out all at once and Naull was left standing with her chemise over her head. She felt her entire, largely exposed body blush as she fumbled with the twisted material. When the garment finally came away from her face, Naull could see Regdar sitting on the floor next to the young woman, whose own skirt had blown scandalously high up her thin, milk-white thighs.

Naull took a deep breath, then felt a chill. Regdar looked up at her and stifled a laugh, his own face turning red. When Naull looked down she realized that the tearing sound had been one of the thin straps of her chemise ripping away. One side of the neckline sagged far enough to reveal what it was intended to hide.

Naull drew the silk over her breast and said, "I ..."

Regdar looked down at the young woman, who was straightening her own garments and breathing heavily. She was beautiful, young, and dressed in fine clothing that was no less attractive for its windblown condition. Her long, blond hair was almost playfully in disarray, a gentle curl falling over her alabaster face, caught up in a diadem knocked askew across her forehead.

Regdar stood, showing an uncharacteristic lack of dexterity, and almost fell on the confused, frightened girl. He reached out and helped her to her feet, quickly withdrawing from her as she shuffled backward toward the door. Her sandaled feet crunched broken glass on the marble.

The girl looked as if she was going to say something but she yelped and jumped back when Regdar's greatsword clattered onto the floor at her feet.

"Naull," Regdar said, his face red, sweaty, and confused, "may I present the duke's daughter, the Lady Maelani."

Naull froze, unable to breathe, think, or move.

Maelani didn't seem any less surprised to see her.

"Are you . . . ?" Maelani said, her voice shaking along with the rest of her. "I mean, is she . . . ? Are you and . . . ?"

Naull stepped closer, still holding her chemise up with one hand, and said, "Why are . . . ? Where did . . . ?"

"Is this . . . ?" Maelani said, looking back and forth between Regdar and Naull. "Are you two . . . ?"

"Does anyone . . . ?" Naull pressed on, wholly unable to synch her mouth with her mind. "Did you . . . ?"

"Please," Regdar cut in, "I think . . ."

"No, it's . . ." Maelani replied.

"It's not . . ." said Naull.

"I mean . . ." Regdar started.

If Naull could have ever imagined an instance in which she'd be happy to have a huge bed flip up off the floor and smash into her back, driving her face-first onto a hard, cold marble floor, this might have been it.

She was unconscious before she knew for sure.

His fighter's instincts took over. Regdar reached out to pull Maelani safely behind him the second the bed came off the floor. Something pushed it up, flipped it over, and took Naull down with it.

Maelani was more fleet of foot than Regdar expected, though, and she flinched just out of his reach. Regdar extended his arm a little too far so that when the edge of the mattress came down on him, his effort to dodge out of the way only sent him sprawling onto the hard, cold floor.

Maelani screamed, and Regdar grunted. There was a loud noise like a door slamming and a deafening rustle of fabric. Regdar saw his sword still on the floor, just within reach, and the backs of Maelani's heels as she scrambled toward the veranda. A heavy blanket and a satin sheet fell over him, blocking his sight, but his hand came down on the hilt of his sword just the same.

A tremendous noise made the floor shake beneath him. Regdar spun on his backside to bring his sword up into a guarding position. He was still under the heavy bedcovers, though, and the fabric twisted around his blade and pressed down against the top of his head as if something heavy held it down.

Maelani screamed again and Regdar heard fabric tear. Through the tight weave of the bedcovers he could see nothing. He scrabbled backward, trying to get out from under the covers and onto his feet at the same time.

He heard Maelani's grunt and the peculiar sound of a body hitting the floor. Regdar growled in frustration as the floor shook again. The bedcovers slipped away and he sensed something coming toward him, something too big to be either Maelani or Naull. Despite years of training to choose his targets carefully, Regdar thrust his greatsword blindly out in front of him.

The tip of the strong, thick blade met resistance. The sword's point tore through the bedcovers and caught on something. There was a scream of metal on metal, and whatever Regdar hit flinched slightly, rolling with the thrust. The blade caught again and Regdar pressed hard, hoping he'd found a space in his unseen opponent's armor. There was a snapping sound and the heavy thing fell away. The sudden release of energy made Regdar lurch forward. He almost succeeded in pushing his own face onto his razor-sharp blade and had to flip himself back equally as violently to avoid it.

There was no tension on the bedcovers. Regdar scrambled to untangle himself, pulling with short jerks in one direction, amazed at how huge an expanse of fabric he was confronted with. He heard a woman moan—it was Maelani—and the sound of something heavy being dragged across the floor.

"Stop!" Regdar shouted, thinking that someone or something was dragging Maelani away.

When the duke's daughter moaned again, from the same place, Regdar knew that wasn't true. He heard a door slam and something heavy and soft sliding across the floor.

The bedcovers finally came off and Regdar grunted, "Damn."

Whatever he'd stabbed was gone. The bed was upside down, but had been slid to one side. He could see the back of Naull's head and her naked back, but the rest of her was still under the bed.

"What . . . ?" Maelani said, and Regdar looked at her.

She was sitting on the floor. Her hair and clothes puffed around her so that she looked both ridiculous and pitiful.

"What was that?" she asked.

"Did you see it?" Regdar asked, crossing to Naull and kneeling next to her.

Maelani shook her head, a tear rolling down one cheek.

"Naull," Regdar whispered.

The young wizard rolled her head to one side and Regdar could see her right eye and the curve of her nose. She blinked and looked up at him.

"Naull?" he prompted again.

"What," she replied, "in the Sand Tombs of Payratheon was that?"

Regdar didn't understand the reference, but was happy to see she was alive. His reply was interrupted by the approaching rumble of what must have been dozens of booted feet.

"Regdar?" Maelani asked, her voice still weak, distant.

He looked at the duke's daughter, sitting there on the floor with her skirts splayed around her, and he swallowed with a dry throat. Regdar could see little reason to believe that anyone knew Maelani had come to visit him. The daughter of the duke of Koratia doesn't go anywhere unannounced, and she sure as the Abyss didn't climb up someone's veranda in the middle of the night unless—

The footsteps were almost at the door when Regdar let his sword clatter to the floor next to Naull. He leaped to his feet and practically fell across the room to Maelani. Still dazed, she didn't try to stop him from scooping her up in his bulky arms.

The footsteps stopped in front of the door and turned to hammering when Regdar deposited Maelani as gently as he could into the room's huge, nearly empty armoire.

"Stay in here," he whispered, "and be quiet."

Maelani nodded and blinked at him. The door to the armoire clicked shut barely a moment before the door to the corridor burst open.

"Lord Constable!" a young city watch sergeant shouted as he stepped into the room.

A dozen of his fellows were behind him, all with swords drawn. They looked around the room with wide, frightened, excited eyes.

"It's gone," Regdar said, noting no small sense of relief from many of the young watchmen.

A signal whistle sounded from behind the shattered windows and Regdar heard the telltale shouts of more watchmen in the street below. The young sergeant walked into the room and sheathed his sword.

Regdar moved to go back to Naull's side, but he kicked something heavy on the floor, stubbing his toe. The object slid a few inches across the polished marble, and Regdar looked at it.

"Lord Constable?" the sergeant asked.

"Lift that bed off her," Regdar ordered as he bent to retrieve the odd bit of twisted metal he'd kicked.

Four of the watchmen moved up and lifted the huge bed off of Naull, who did her best to crawl out from under it.

"Regdar," she called, "where's—?"

He held up a hand to silence her and they shared a look. He was gratified to see that Naull understood the greater implications of a detachment of city watchmen finding the duke's daughter in the Lord Constable's bedchamber, with Naull no less.

As Naull freed herself from the bed, Regdar examined the chunk of metal. It was gray, dull steel of the sort often used for armor.

"What is it?" the watch sergeant asked.

"A piece of the killer's armor," Regdar said, though he suspected that was not the whole story.

The sergeant seemed about to reply when he was interrupted by a shrill, lewd whistle.

"Nice," Naull scowled.

Regdar looked over and saw that she had made it out from under the overturned bed, but her silk chemise hadn't.

"Sergeant," Regdar said, "will you take your men into the hall and give the lady some privacy, please?"

Blushing, the young sergeant reluctantly complied.

Naull had never dressed so fast in her life. She was hardly a vain woman, but she liked to put some thought into her wardrobe. As Regdar coaxed a quivering Maelani out of the armoire, though, Naull just threw on whatever was at hand. She stopped for a breath only after finally slinging her pouches over her shoulder.

"What happened?" Maelani asked Regdar.

Naull stepped toward them more forcefully than she should have. There was something about Maelani's body language that made it obvious she wanted Regdar to take her into his arms. The beautiful young woman leaned into him, seemed almost on the verge of collapsing.

Naull took her by the arm, startling her.

"I'll get you out of here," the wizard said.

"But . . ." Maelani started, looking at Regdar.

Naull pulled on the girl's arm and said, "The lord constable has work to do."

Regdar, still blushing, unable or unwilling to look either woman in the eye, said, "Naull will take good care of you."

Maelani shook her head, but let Naull pull her a few steps farther away from Regdar.

The fighter crossed to the overturned bed and looked down at the floor. Naull followed his eyes and saw the hole in the marble. It was big—easily big enough for all three of them to drop through at the same time. The bed would have rested right over the hole. Whatever flipped it off the floor had obviously come up through there.

"I can't imagine this has been here the whole time," Regdar said, speaking more to himself than to either Naull or Maelani.

Naull was about to make a suggestion when a loud knock sounded again at the door.

"Lord Constable," the watch sergeant barked, "if the lady is no longer ... indisposed, perhaps we should conduct an investigation?"

Regdar looked at Naull, then at Maelani. He seemed at a loss.

"Where does that hole lead to?" Naull asked in a whisper as she dragged Maelani around the overturned bed.

"The room downstairs," Regdar said, peering into the hole. "Looks like there's another hole just like it in the floor there, and another ... into, what, the basement or wine cellar or something?"

Naull stopped at the edge of the hole and swallowed. Her head spun, and she almost fainted.

After a deep, cleansing sigh, she said, "Lower us down."

Regdar lifted an eyebrow, but finally looked her in the eye.

"I know," she said, "but it's the best way out of here without your men seeing Maelani."

"My men?" Regdar asked, then he shook his head. "Oh, yes ... my men."

The big fighter bent and grabbed the strong satin sheet.

"Lord Constable?" the sergeant called from the hallway.

"One minute," Regdar answered as he started wrapping the big sheet into an improvised rope.

"Heights," Naull said, peering down into the thankfully vacant room below. "Always heights. . . ."

Naull and Maelani walked out of the Thrush and the Jay past a crowd of watchmen. The constables were, by then, looking for something big, heavy, and armored, so the two slight women in their city clothes and close-drawn cowls easily passed unnoticed.

Once out of the inn, they crossed the street without speaking and silently slipped into the late night shadows.

"You managed to sneak out of the palace," Naull said at last, her voice barely above a whisper, "but did you have a plan for getting back in?"

Maelani looked at her, one eye peeking out from the edge of her cowl. The look was hard, accusatory, but at the same time fragile and embarrassed. Naull was briefly taken aback by the strong emotions the girl radiated. It had been some time since Naull had been with another young woman, and she'd grown accustomed not only to the company of men but the quiet stoicism of Regdar and adventurers like him.

They came to the end of the street, and the brightly-lit marketplace stretched out ahead of them. The huge dome of the Wizard's Horde glittered across the street. To their left was the bridge that would take Maelani back to her island palace. The guards standing at the foot of the bridge were plainly visible, as were their razor-sharp halberds that glowed with obvious magic.

The two women stopped on the corner, and Maelani drew her cowl even closer around her face. She met Naull's eyes.

"I was," she whispered, "not informed of . . . I didn't know that the lord constable was married. Please forgive me."

Naull held back a laugh, but not a smile.

"We're not married," she said. "We are sharing the room, though, as we have shared many things."

"I didn't go there to . . ." the young lady said, then she turned away.

Naull touched her elbow and gently drew her back so they could see each others' faces again.

"Your father knows about me," she said. "If he's pressuring you, as he's pressuring Regdar, I . . ."

Maelani tipped her head to one side, waiting for Naull to finish. The mage just sighed and looked down.

Naull felt warm, thin fingers touch her chin. It was Maelani's turn to bring the mage's eyes back to her own.

"I love my father," she said. "He is the best man I have ever known, and he has raised me well. His example has made me more demanding of young men than some girls can be. He isn't pressuring me or Regdar but if he gives an order, I, like the lord constable, will follow it."

Naull almost flinched from the cool challenge in the young woman's eyes.

"Not all of the duke's subjects are willing to set their private lives aside for his whims," Naull said, not sure herself where the conversation was heading. "Love, as they say, conquers all."

Maelani smiled. To Naull the expression seemed sincere, friendly.

"I was surprised to see you there," Maelani said.

Naull returned her smile and replied, "And I thought you were the murderer."

"No," Maelani said, "but I get the feeling you'd have been happier if I had been."

Naull felt the fine hairs on the back of her neck bristle and she said, "Not at all, Lady Maelani. If you were the murderer, Regdar and I would have to kill you. As it stands—"

"As it stands," Maelani interrupted, "you may want to anyway."

"He loves me," Naull blurted.

The wizard felt her cheeks flare red, but she kept her eyes on Maelani's.

The girl smiled, but the expression was a bit crooked this time.

"The bridge guards can see me from here," the duke's daughter said. "I won't be bothered by this murderer again tonight."

Naull tipped her head in agreement but kept her eyes on the girl's.

"I hope you and the lord constable can find this . . . thing, before anyone else is hurt," Maelani said, "but I also hope you'll continue to cover for me."

"You should stay in the palace," Naull said, more quickly and harshly than she'd intended. "Until the murderer is caught, it's the only place your safety can be assured."

Maelani nodded once and said, "I guess that means we shan't ever see one another again."

Naull tried to smile, but succeeded only in grimacing.

This made Maelani smile, and she was still smiling even as Naull stood there on the corner, watching her go.

Regdar couldn't have been more relieved when Naull and Maelani crept out the door of the room below and he was finally able to let the watchmen back in. The surprising appearance of Maelani had thrown him more off-balance than he would have imagined. Regdar wanted to believe that Naull didn't think he and the girl had planned it. Regdar wanted to tell Naull in no uncertain terms that he had no interest in Maelani and did nothing to encourage her to sneak into his bedchamber in the middle of the night. He hadn't had the chance, though, with the duke's daughter there the whole time. Turning Maelani away could easily be seen as an insult to the duke himself, and Regdar would die before he'd do such a thing—yet he had little choice.

"Lord Constable?" the sergeant prodded, breaking Regdar from his confusing, circular ruminations.

"Yes," Regdar replied, though he hadn't heard the question.

The sergeant narrowed his eyes in confusion and was about to speak when he was interrupted by a call from below. Both Regdar and the sergeant stepped to the edge of the hole and looked down. Two watchmen stood in the room below, one looking up at his sergeant, the other down the hole in that room's floor.

"The innkeeper says this room's vacant," the watchman reported. "Should I have a look around?"

Before the sergeant could answer, Regdar said, "No. Touch nothing. I want to examine it myself, and I will have a mage examine it as well."

The watchman nodded and said, "Yes, Lord Constable."

Lord Constable, Regdar thought. Duke . . . "What have I gotten myself into?"

"I'm sorry, sir?" the sergeant asked.

Regdar shook off the question, barely aware that he'd muttered that last bit aloud.

"Goes all the way down!" a voice echoed up from below.

Regdar looked down again and saw another pair of watchmen in the ground floor room, two stories below.

"What's below you?" Regdar called down.

Both of them looked around, then one called up, "Looks like a pantry or something. I see sacks of rice and flour and some crates."

"There will be a door down there," Regdar told the sergeant, "but one not easily recognizable."

"A secret door?" the sergeant asked. "Are you sure?"

Regdar thought of Naull's spellcasting the day before and nodded.

"One of my men's a half-elf," the sergeant said. "He's got an eye for that sort of thing."

Regdar nodded and the sergeant slipped away to give the order.

"Nice work, anyway," one of the watchmen called up.

"What was that?" Regdar asked.

"The carving," a watchman in the room below replied, pointing at the holes in the marble floors. "It was expertly done, I can tell you that."

Regdar crouched and ran a fingertip along the smooth, rounded edge of the hole. The floors were solid marble. The place was more regally built than Regdar imagined. It must have taken magic to lay those slabs and probably to cut them so perfectly in the first place.

"I used to work with my uncle," the watchman continued from below, "carving headstones. Depressing work, and I didn't have a talent for it like he did."

"This would take time, wouldn't it?" Regdar said. "Work like this through, what, six inches or more of solid marble?"

The watchman nodded and said, "My uncle could have done it, when he was alive. It would take him the better part of a month, and you'd sure as mages mumble have been able to hear him working at it."

The floors were kept polished by the Thrush and the Jay's dedicated cleaning staff. As Regdar felt the edge of the hole, he thought he felt ripples, like ridges or depressions.

"Fingers," he said aloud.

"Sorry, lord?" the watchman below asked.

"Nothing," Regdar said. "Best get you two out of there and seal the room. I want you four to guard those rooms, two on each door. No one goes in without my orders."

The watchmen in the rooms below made various signals and grunts of understanding, and disappeared from Regdar's view.

Regdar stood but his eyes roamed the edges of the hole. He couldn't shake the feeling that he'd seen something like that edge before, and his mind wandered to his mother's pottery wheel. He hadn't thought about that in a long time, but he could see her fingers press gently into the wet, turning clay.

With a sigh, Regdar drew the jagged piece of steel from his pocket and eyed it.

"Who are you?" he whispered, "and how did you work solid marble like it was soft clay?"

And why, he asked silently, were you trying to kill the duke's daughter?

"Damn it!" Vargussel swore. "Damn it all to the Hubs of Hell!"

He picked up a chair, one of the few functional pieces of furniture in the room, and did his best to hurl it at the wall. The chair clattered to the floor, splashing into a puddle of fetid muck.

Vargussel put his hands to his temples and pressed. His head throbbed, his jaw was taut, and he thought his eyes might pop out of his head. He heard the shield guardian stomp into the confines of his secret laboratory but Vargussel didn't turn around to look at it.

Opening his eyes, he crossed to the elaborate stand on which rested a crystal ball. He touched the medallion that hung around his neck and silently commanded the shield guardian to take its usual place against the far wall. The construct complied without question.

"Damn you," Vargussel spat into the crystal ball.

Floating in the clear, colorless glass was an image of the basement of the Thrush and the Jay. Light spilled into the room from above where the shield guardian had shaped a hole in the ceiling. Vargussel had spent most of the night patting himself on the back for his genius. The shield guardian had the power to store a single spell and use it at Vargussel's command. The spell he'd equipped the construct with that night allowed it to work the solid marble of the inn's floors as if it was soft butter. The shield guardian tunneled its way straight up to the new Lord Constable's bedchamber, the element of surprise intact. The construct had been in the room for only seconds before Vargussel had stopped patting himself on the back.

How could Vargussel have known the Lord Constable wouldn't be alone?

Vargussel rested his hands on the cool surface of the crystal ball and sighed, trying to calm himself.

"You nearly killed her," he muttered to the construct standing silently behind him.

Vargussel took his hands away from the crystal when he saw two men dressed in the tabards of the city watch cautiously step into view. Their swords were drawn, and their eyes were wide with fearful expectation.

"It's long gone, you fools," the mage said to the gently glowing image.

The watchmen had no reaction. They couldn't hear him. Vargussel could see into the inn's basement from the safety of the abandoned slaughterhouse but the soldiers would never know they were being watched. Vargussel didn't bother noting details about the two watchmen. They would either find the secret door or not.

"Try to find me from there," the mage mumbled, confident that the maze of sewer tunnels between the inn and the slaughterhouse would provide adequate protection from simple city watchmen.

One of the watchmen searched the wall dangerously close to the secret door, but still he hadn't see it.

"Oh, you're good," the mage grumbled.

Vargussel noted the gently rounded point at the top of the watchman's ears, the fair complexion, the pale green eyes . . . a half-elf.

"Well," Vargussel said with a wry laugh, "here they co—"

The crystal ball shattered in his face. It exploded into a cloud of razor-sharp shards so quickly and abruptly, the mage only barely had time to shield his eyes.

Vargussel threw himself back and landed hard on a pile of rotting lumber. A big, mangy rat squealed loudly and scurried from the pile, jumping over one of Vargussel's legs in its hurry to get away. The mage flinched away from the rat, then kicked at it. The rodent was long gone through a hole in the tumble-down walls.

"A new pet, Vargussel?" a familiar voice rumbled through the laboratory.

With a gasp, Vargussel whirled at the sound. In the air above him the shards of crystal had coalesced into a floating cloud of glittering slivers. The cloud took the shape of a man's face, its features smooth and ill-defined, though Vargussel knew exactly who it was. The floating image turned its attention on the cowering mage, who scrambled into a deep, groveling bow.

"Great One!" the mage simpered.

"Silence, servant," the image boomed. "Listen and learn."

Vargussel clenched his teeth to keep from talking or babbling in the face of the crystal image.

"Your progress is slow," the image said.

There was a pause and Vargussel looked up, still clenching his teeth, and raised an eyebrow for some sign as to whether the image required an answer.

"I believed in you," the image said, and Vargussel bent his neck again, scraping his forehead on the ground. "You persuaded me."

There was another pause, but Vargussel didn't look up.

"Speak!" the image roared, sending a tinkling spray of broken glass showering harmlessly over the groveling mage.

"The plan is moving forward, O Great One!" Vargussel shouted back. "Trust in me. I will not fail you. The girl will be mine, then the city, then the duchy will be yours. This I swear by the Many-Headed Hydra in the Center of the—"

"Enough!"

Vargussel wrapped his arms over his head and pressed his face into the rotting floorboards.

"Time passes, Vargussel," the image said. "Time passes quickly."

Vargussel held his breath and pressed his eyes closed at the sound of the thousands of shards of crystal raining down around him. He felt nothing, though, and after a few heartbeats had passed without another word from the image, he dared open one eye and look up.

The crystal ball sat on the pedestal again, intact and unmarred. In it was an image of the half-elf watchman waving his friend forward. The watchman said something to his companion that Vargussel couldn't hear, and the other man ran back up the basement stairs.

Vargussel touched the medallion at his neck and said, "Awaken."

The shield guardian lurched forward and stood ready as Vargussel watched the half-elf silently trace the top of a finger around the hairline crack that marked his secret door.

"Start clearing out this place," Vargussel told the construct. "Should they manage to find it, I want it to be empty and useless to them."

"Here, Lord Constable," the half-elf said as he crossed the basement floor and indicated a blank space on the wall.

"Show me," Regdar said, squinting at the wall but seeing no sign of a door.

The half-elf traced a straight line with the tip of a finger and Regdar stepped up to the wall. He had to lean in so close to the wall to see it his nose almost touched the rough masonry. There was a crack, no wider than the width of a single hair, but as the half-elf traced its shape Regdar saw it more clearly. The crack outlined the rectangular shape of a low, wide door.

"There's no handle," Regdar said. "How do we open it?"

"I've been working on that, Lord Constable," the half-elf replied, "but I can't find a catch or trigger or anything."

Regdar nodded and stepped back to survey the wall.

"We'll need more light," he said over his shoulder to the young sergeant waiting behind him. "Have lanterns brought in, and bring as many crowbars as you can find ... and a pick and shovel."

The young sergeant nodded and hurried off.

"We're going to pry it open, my lord?" the half-elf asked.

Regdar shrugged and replied, "Unless you find a better way through before those crowbars get here."

The half-elf nodded, taking the hint, and went back to his close examination of the secret door. Regdar used the time to survey the hole in the ceiling, marveling at the fact that he could see clear up to the ceiling of the room he shared with Naull.

When the sergeant returned a short time later with a few more men and the necessary tools, Regdar looked at the half-elf with one eyebrow arched.

The half-elf shrugged, shook his head, and stepped aside. Regdar put out a hand and the sergeant set a crowbar across his palm.

"Three men with me," he said, quickly counting five watchmen in the basement, "the other two stand ready with weapons drawn."

One of the younger watchmen swallowed and drew his sword in a shaking hand.

"Do you . . . ?" the young man asked. "Do you think it's still in there?"

Regdar found the hairline crack, set the end of his crowbar in it, and said, "No."

He heard at least three of the watchmen sigh with relief, heard a second blade drawn, and the sergeant and two of his men pressed their own crowbars into the skinny crack.

It took them several minutes just to chip away at the surrounding mortar enough to get their crowbars set. When the three watchmen nodded to Regdar in turn that they were ready, the lord constable gave the order and they pushed. Regdar didn't put all his strength into the first attempt, in case the crowbar wasn't as firmly set or the wall as well-mortared as he thought. The crowbar dug into the crack but the door didn't budge.

"Are you set well?" he asked the other three. They nodded and Regdar turned his head to address the two men with swords. "I'm sure it's long gone by now, men, but look alive just the same."

The two guards swallowed and nodded. They held their swords in a ready position, their feet set wide apart. Regdar turned back to the door and tightened his grip on the crowbar.

"On three, then," he said. "One . . . two . . . three!"

They pushed with all their might, and at first it seemed as if they were trying to move a mountain. When Regdar felt the crowbar move, he backed off, thinking it had slipped from the crack and not wanting to accidentally injure one of the other men.

"It's . . . opening," the sergeant grunted.

Regdar blinked at the crack. It was indeed wider than it had been when the half-elf first found it.

"Put your backs into it," he ordered, then did the same himself.

With considerable effort, the four of them worked their crowbars deeper into the space between the door and the wall. When Regdar thought it felt as if the door was going to come open, he stopped pushing and held up a hand. The others stopped and Regdar motioned for them to back up.

"It's almost there," he said, gesturing to two of the men. "You two, stand on either side, watch your toes, and push. Sergeant . . ."

The sergeant dropped his crowbar and stepped back, drawing his sword. Regdar let his own crowbar clatter to the flagstone floor and slipped his greatsword from its sheath on his back. When both he and the sergeant were matching the other two watchmen's stance, Regdar nodded to the men with crowbars.

They pressed their backs into it with impressive will and surprising strength. All the while, Regdar tried to trace the outline of the door and match its size and shape to the floor in front of him. When the section of brick wall came out, it was likely going to fall, and any toes that strayed under it would be lost for good.

"Careful, now," he cautioned, though both men had their feet well back.

The door came loose all at once, but seemed to hang in the air for a precarious second. The two men with crowbars leaped to either side as the section of brick started slowly, gently tipping into the room.

With both hands on his sword, Regdar couldn't hold his hands over his ears, though he knew he should. If he had, though, he wouldn't have heard the footsteps on the stairs behind him. Thinking at first that his men were deserting, Regdar spun to face the stairs while the secret door fell, revealing a dark space beyond.

Torn between the footsteps that were descending the stairs—his men were still standing ready—and the darkness beyond the secret door, Regdar wasn't sure where to turn, so he whipped his head back and forth trying to see both sides at once. This startled his men, who looked at him, then whipped their heads forward when the heavy section of brick wall hit the flagstones with a thunderous boom that shook the floor and sent up a cloud of dust and pebbles of brick and mortar.

The tall, skinny man who ran the inn slipped down the stairs at what appeared to be an all-out run. Recognizing him right away, Regdar put his full attention back to the yawning, black hole in the wall. His ears were ringing and the bottoms of his feet tingled from the vibration of the floor, but he was ready for anything.

He counted three fast heartbeats, and nothing came out of the darkness but a rotten, dank smell of decay.

"What is the meaning of this?" the tall man said, breaking the silence that had descended over Regdar and his men.

Regdar relaxed his stance and turned to the innkeeper slowly, keeping his sword at his side in an unthreatening manner.

"You're the innkeeper," he said.

The man sketched a shallow bow, his face flashing from anger to surprise to anger again, and back to surprise in the course of a second.

"I am Feargal Haelliuzh," the man said, "proprietor of the Thrush and the Jay, and I am at your service, Lord Constable."

Regdar didn't bother wondering how the innkeeper knew of his appointment.

"Did you know about this?" Regdar asked.

The innkeeper shook his head, his eyes wide, his hands turning palm up.

"The secret door," Regdar said. "Did you know this was here?"

"No," said Haelliuzh.

Regdar saw the half-elf kneel in front of the fallen door and examine its edges, but he turned his attention back to the innkeeper.

"We will need to seal off the basement as well," Regdar said.

"But, Lord Constable, I . . ." the innkeeper began.

Regdar tipped his head to one side and lifted an eyebrow, and the tall man bowed deeply.

"My most sincere apologies, Lord Constable," he said. "Of course, the Thrush and the Jay is forever at the duke's disposal."

"Thank you," Regdar said. "If your people need anything from down here, just have them ask one of the guards and he'll have it brought up."

"Most gracious of you," Haelliuzh replied. The innkeeper looked around one last time and said, "I will leave you to your work then."

Regdar nodded and the man was gone in a flash.

"Well," the half-elf said, fingering a twisted bit of metal sticking out of the side of the fallen door, "here's the catch."

Regdar barely glanced at the ruin of the elaborate hinge and spring-clasp left twisted and ruined by their crowbars. Instead, he stepped to the edge of the dark space and eased his head through the doorway. The opening led to a wide, dark shaft that plunged into the ground past the reach of the light filtering in from the basement. The shaft ran straight down into the sewers. Though Regdar couldn't see the bottom of the shaft, he knew a sewer when he smelled one.

The stench was strong. Still holding his greatsword, Regdar put up one hand to cover his nose.

"The sewers," he announced.

Regdar saw a steel rung mortared into the wall behind and below the opening. The steel rung was the top of a ladder that was built into the wall of the shaft. From below, Regdar could hear the sound of rushing water echoing in the sewers far below.

Nothing else moved or made a sound.

"Do we go down?" the sergeant asked him.

Regdar turned, having quickly made up his mind.

"Not yet," said the lord constable. "Whatever that was, it was big, and we'll be in its territory. We know how it moves now, but there's an awful lot of sewer down there. We need a map, a plan, a mage maybe . . . weapons and supplies for sure."

"But we are going in?" the sergeant asked, his voice quiet, almost tentative.

Regdar looked at him and smiled.

Maelani turned left onto the paved walkway along the strand and sighed in relief when the Thrush and the Jay hid her from Naull's view. She wasn't sure, but Maelani thought she could feel the woman's eyes follow her all the way down the street. It was a risk turning off the road before she was confronted by the bridge guards, but if they saw her face, she would have to answer to her father.

She ambled along the path with the cowl pulled over her head, trying for all she was worth to appear casual, just a young woman out for a pre-dawn stroll. That was strange enough, even in one of the city's better neighborhoods, but all she needed was to avoid both the bridge guards and Naull long enough to get back into the inn.

A small crowd of watchmen milled about the strand, most of them still looking up at the broken windows of Regdar's room. The memory of floating up to that balcony, propelled by her enchanted sandals, made Maelani momentarily dizzy. She walked slowly, eyeing the guards from the shadows of her cloak. When none of them were looking directly at her, she slipped into the deep shadows of the inn's columned patio.

One of the Thrush and the Jay's house guards was lighting lamps in a line along the wall. Intent on his work, and made nightblind by the lamps only inches from his face, he never saw Maelani step into a curtained alcove.

Reserved for the inn's most privacy-conscious clientele, the alcoves were often rented by the month. Maelani, through her maid, had rented one almost a year before under an assumed name. She paid well for it, having to sell some of her jewelry and trading a favor or two. The portal had cost her even more.

A three-month-old baby was being raised in the Trade Quarter by a peasant couple who managed to make a fortune when they both discovered they had dragon blood and a talent for sorcery. Something in their past made it impossible (at least in their own minds) for them to ascend to the aristocracy, but they purchased the title, held in trust, for their baby when he came of age.

The title was a small thing for Maelani but huge for the family of sorcerers, and it bought her the portal in secrecy.

Pausing in the utter darkness of the alcove, Maelani took a deep breath.

"Regdar," she whispered, then quickly put a hand to her lips.

The place was still crawling with guards and she didn't want to be found, but she didn't want to go home, either. She came to the Thrush and the Jay that night with a purpose, and her mission had been interrupted.

Maelani pushed away the memory of the bed exploding at her, the bedcovers, the stomping, the fear of something lumbering toward her. Instead, she let her thoughts fill with the feeling of Regdar's arms around her, of the lord constable picking her up like she was a baby, and of his cool, confident gaze as he lowered her and the other woman down through the hole in the floor.

Here was a man truly worthy of the duchy and of her, but he was with that peasant, that trollop, that street mage.

Maelani felt her jaw tense with anger, embarrassment, and jealousy.

She thinks he loves her, Maelani thought, and maybe he does, but we haven't been alone yet.

Maelani thought of the potion, and her face relaxed. She wouldn't use it unless she had to, and she truly didn't think she had to, Naull or no Naull, but it was nice to know she had it just in case.

With a smile, she stepped onto an enchanted floor tile, whispered a command word, and faded from the pitch-dark alcove.

Regdar stretched, holding his neck. He hadn't slept and the adrenaline high that followed the mysterious attack had long since run its course. While he was still gathering men and resources to begin a search of the sewers, Naull returned. She'd said only a few words to him about having to rest and regain her spells. She seemed angry, but maybe scared as well. The look on her face and the tone of her voice troubled Regdar deeply, but as always seemed to be the case, he had pressing work to do, more immediate problems, and Naull would have to wait—and understand.

Standing knee-deep in waste water, Regdar finished stretching and pressed on. The tracker was several paces ahead of him, and already there was a space of inky darkness between the pools of light from his lantern and Regdar's. The curved ceiling was only a few inches over Regdar's head, and the walls were only a couple feet to either side of him. The sewer passage was a long, brickwork cylinder—a pipe, really. Sounds echoed so strangely in its confines that Regdar eventually gave up jumping at every sudden noise. A drip could sound like a war-horse's hooves, a splash like the beating of a giant heart.

The tracker was another of the city watchmen who Regdar commanded, though he hadn't met the man an hour before. The sergeant told him that the tracker, whose name was Willis, had worked in the sewers and knew their quirks. Having spent an hour following Willis through the worst place in New Koratia, Regdar wasn't so sure. They seemed to just be walking in a straight line.

Behind him followed two more watchmen, whispering gripes and dirty jokes to each other to pass the time. Regdar wished he could join them but he was still working out how a Lord Constable should act, and griping with the men probably wasn't it.

He had three more teams of four men apiece fanned out in the maze of sewer tunnels, each led by someone who claimed to know the subterranean ins and outs. Regdar could only hope that one of those other teams, at least, was on the right track.

He was beginning to think about turning his team around and going back to the Thrush and the Jay when one of the men behind him screamed. Regdar whirled and saw a single, flailing arm surrounded by splashing water. The other watchman moved back and to the side, pushing through the water, pinwheeling his arms so that the sword in his right hand scraped the ceiling and the wall close behind him.

Regdar sloshed toward the commotion, scanning the rippling water for the downed man. Bits of garbage and feces bobbed in the brown water, which was being churned from below. The water was no more than two feet deep, and Regdar couldn't believe the watchman could have disappeared completely in it.

"What happened?" he asked the missing man's partner.

The watchman looked at him with wild eyes and managed to say, "He just—" before the water exploded up into Regdar's face, and the missing man appeared with a high-pitched, gurgling scream.

The horrible sound echoed over and over again in the sewer tunnel, and Regdar bent back away from the man's fear-ravaged face as it lunged toward him, or was pushed at him. Something had the man in its jaws.

"Run!" the tracker called.

Regdar grabbed at the flailing man and got hold of his soaking tabard. The fabric tore, and the man was jerked back. Something slapped the water, and the light dimmed in the tunnel when the lantern was knocked out of Regdar's hand by the screaming watchman's flailing hands.

It was a snake that had him—a huge snake with a head as big as the watchman's torso.

The snake dropped its head and the still flailing watchman back into the water. It slithered forward under the surface. Regdar felt it slide across his legs, then it twitched against him and almost pushed him off his feet.

Regdar drew his sword but momentarily forgot the low ceiling. The heavy blade clanged against the bricks.

The tracker was trying to run away and was still loudly urging the others to do the same when either the drowning victim or the monster snake itself tripped him up. He fell facefirst, his lantern dropping into the water with him and going out. The only light left was one small lantern held by the man who'd watched his partner fall to the snake, and that man was taking the tracker's advice. He was running away as fast as he could manage in the knee-deep water and taking the only remaining light with him.

"Stop!" Regdar shouted at the man's receding back.

Regdar looked back over his shoulder and saw the disturbance in the water as the snake slithered away just under the surface. The tracker splashed past him, and they made eye contact as he went by. Regdar saw a little guilt there, but not much. There was another splash from farther up the tunnel and the snake's victim screamed again.

Regdar reached out to grab the tracker but the man stopped anyway, looking back at his dying comrade.

"Your bow," Regdar said, keeping his hand out.

Willis slipped the shortbow off his shoulder and handed it to Regdar, who took the liberty of sliding an arrow out of the tracker's quiver. He nocked the arrow and drew back the string in a single motion. He aimed but the light was already so far behind him that he was basically shooting blind.

"Pin it," the tracker said, and Regdar let the arrow fly.

There was a great disturbance in the water—splashing, a cough, something like a shout—and the light didn't get any dimmer. The other watchman started splashing his way back.

"Did you get it?" the man called. "Did he get it?"

"Help!" came echoing down the corridor, then was swallowed up by more splashing.

"He got it," Willis said, and followed Regdar up the tunnel.

"Get him to the temple," Regdar said as he handed the wounded man to a pair of watchmen in the basement of the Thrush and the Jay.

The remaining two members of Regdar's team clanged up the ladder behind him as the wounded man was carried away, bleeding, his head lolling weakly to one side.

"You found it," Naull said, and Regdar flinched.

He hadn't expected to see her there, but was instantly happy he did. She was dressed in her traveling clothes, with her straps of pouches over her shoulders and her hair tied up away from her face.

"What was it?" she asked.

"It was a snake," he said.

"A dire snake," the tracker Willis added as he climbed through the formerly secret door behind Regdar. "A nasty one, too. Almost swallowed Kirk whole."

Regdar found himself about to ask who Kirk was, then realized he needed to start introducing himself to his men. He was ordering them into the notoriously dangerous city sewers and hadn't even bothered to learn their names.

"A snake?" Naull asked, skeptical.

She had good instincts.

"It was just a big snake," Regdar said, "that lives in the sewers. It wasn't what tunneled up and tried to kill M—" he almost said Maelani but quickly switched to—"me. It was just an animal."

"A *big* animal," said the fourth member of Regdar's team as he crawled from the shaft.

"So, you didn't find it," Naull said.

Regdar opened his mouth to reply, but the sergeant spoke first.

"One of the other teams got a good trail."

Regdar looked at him and asked, "What trail?"

"Scratches on the ceiling," the sergeant reported, "fresh and deep."

"Where?" Regdar asked.

A watchman covered in dirty water and filth stepped up from behind the sergeant and said, "Goes right out to the river, My Lord. It's only a couple hundred feet really, but I had a hunch, so we got a boat, rowed across, and went in through an opening on the eastern bank. We followed the scratches deep into the Trade Quarter but lost the trail in a particularly nasty stretch, one that runs under where the old slaughterhouse is. I heard they were going to pull it down but for now, it's just a smelly, old eyesore. No one ever goes near it—at least, no one with a nose."

"A good place to hide," Regdar said. "Good work, Constable . . . ?"

"Jandik," the man replied.

"Constable Jandik," Regdar said. "Draw some fresh men and supplies and another boat. I trust you can find this slaughterhouse again."

"Yes, My Lord."

As Jandik trundled up the stairs out of the basement, Regdar fished in a pouch for the piece of jagged metal he'd cut from the intruder. He found it and handed it to Naull.

"What's this?" she asked.

"A piece of whatever it was that came up from under the bed."

She frowned and turned it over in her hand.

"Is there a spell," he asked, "that could tell you what that was or what it came from?"

She looked at the metal fragment in her hand with renewed interest, then looked off, thinking.

"Naull," Regdar said, taking her by the arm and leading her away from the other men, "I never got a chance to——"

She jerked her arm away and said, "Yes."

A few of the watchmen looked over at them, but when Regdar met their gazes, they turned away.

"Yes," Naull continued in a quieter voice, "there is a spell, but I don't know it. My mentor called it 'legend lore.'"

"Sergeant," Regdar called without turning away from Naull.

The young sergeant came up behind him, and Regdar said, "This is Naull, a mage in whom I place the utmost trust. Escort her to the palace im——"

"I'm not going to the palace," Naull interrupted. Regdar raised an eyebrow and she continued. "You need me with you when you go to that slaughterhouse. If the duke has someone who can cast that spell, he doesn't need me, but you might."

Regdar smiled but Naull didn't. He got the idea she was trying hard not to.

"Sergeant," Regdar said, taking the piece of metal from Naull's hand, "what's your name?"

"Lorec, My Lord," the sergeant said. "Watch Sergeant Lorec."

Regdar held the piece of metal out to the man and said, "Watch Sergeant Lorec, I'm trusting you to convey this directly to the duke. Ask him to call on wizards that he trusts to cast this . . ."

"Legend lore," Naull provided.

"As quickly as possible," finished Regdar.

Lorec took the jagged shard and said, "Yes, Lord Constable."

Naull drew her cloak tighter around her neck and shivered against the chill wind. The weather had taken a decided turn for the worse, and threatening black clouds loomed in the west. Already, the young mage could feel the chill pinpoints of rain on her face. The cold water of the River Delnir reflected the gray sky and the sight of it only made Naull shiver again.

The boat rode low in the water, weighed down by Regdar and his men. The watchmen were dressed in full plate armor and carried long swords and longbows. Some of the younger ones shivered as well, from the cold and wet at least, but likely with fear as well. Four of them worked the heavy oars, and they crossed the wide river at a good pace, considering the speed of the southward current they had to fight the whole way. Crossing from west to east, passing the southern point of the Duke's Quarter, they at least had the growing wind at their backs.

Constable Jandik, the tracker who found the trail left by the monster, sat in the bow of the boat, guiding the oarsmen toward a gaping, black hole in the high river wall. Naull sat next to Lorec, the young watch sergeant who had gathered the other four watchmen at Regdar's command. Regdar stood on the bow next to

Jandik, looking for all the world like some grand admiral leading his armada to victory.

He likes it, she thought. He's settling into this new life of his, and he loves every minute of it. Maybe Maelani was—

Naull shook her head, dislodging the thought, and tried to concentrate on the task ahead.

As they approached the river wall, Naull noticed some of the men making signs and gestures surely meant to ward off evil spirits. All of them eyed the building at the top of the river wall with apprehension if not terror.

It was a huge manor house of sprawling wings, high turrets, and wide verandas. Whoever lived there must have been the envy of any of the duchy's wealthiest families.

"Haunted," Lorec whispered in her ear, startling her. "I'm sorry, ma'am. I saw you looking at the mansion."

"It's beautiful," Naull said.

"It is," replied Lorec, "and people pay a pretty penny to stay there. It's sort of a high-class boarding house. Personally, I wouldn't spend a night there if my life de—"

He stopped when the boat nudged up against the river wall. Regdar reached up and grabbed a rusted iron rung, and Jandik handed him a rope. As Regdar tied the boat to the ladder, Naull looked up at the circle of blackness that marked the entrance to the sewers.

"Look alive, men," Lorec called to his watchmen, who were already stowing their oars.

Thunder rumbled in the distance and Naull shivered again. She had to bite her tongue not to call out to Regdar to stop. He was already scaling the ladder to the sewer entrance with his mighty greatsword swinging from his back. Naull had a very, very bad feeling about that sewer.

Regdar peeked into the sewer from the bottom edge of the opening while trying not to look like he was peeking. It seemed to

Regdar that a Lord Constable shouldn't peek, but stride confidently into any situation. Regdar was too smart for that.

There was nothing in the immediate vicinity of the entrance, so he drew himself up the rest of the way and stopped when his knee rested on the edge of the opening. He tried to listen but all he could hear was echoes from the boat tapping the river wall and the boatload of watchmen gathering their gear.

Regdar looked back over his shoulder and caught Lorec's eye.

"It's narrow," the lord constable said, "so we'll have to walk single-file. I want Jandik in front—" the tracker nodded—"then myself. Naull, you stick behind me and be ready with those spells. Behind Naull I want Samoth with sword and lantern, then Lorec, then Lem and Asil, all three with bows. Drahir, you have the rear with lantern and sword."

Each of the men nodded in turn, and Regdar leaned to the side to allow Jandik to scramble up into the sewer entrance past him. He drew his greatsword and followed the tracker into the sewer, clearing the entrance for the others.

Regdar had taken the time to learn the names and even some of the strengths and weaknesses of the men Lorec had gathered. They seemed fit enough, but only time would tell. Regdar had been in enough battles with soldiers both green and veteran to know that each man would perform in his own way. Some would never be meant for combat while others would take to it like he had. Unfortunately, there was only one way to find out for sure.

He helped Naull up into the sewer and said, "Are you all right?"

The question offended her but Regdar didn't care. She seemed worried.

"I'm fine," she said, "but I'm not sure why we're going this way. If we know the trail leads to an abandoned slaughterhouse, why not just go there? Why creep around in darkness and filth?"

Regdar waved her deeper into the sewer to allow watchman Samoth to get in after her.

"I did send a contingent to the slaughterhouse," he said. "They're likely there already. This is the way the creature, or whatever it is, moves. It may not be in the slaughterhouse itself, and if it's chased out by the men on the ground, it'll likely run this way—into us."

He could see her swallow hard.

"That doesn't make me feel any better," she said.

They kept moving deeper into the stinking, black tunnel as the rest of their party climbed in and lanterns were lit.

"Don't tell me you aren't itching for revenge," Regdar prodded. "If somebody flipped a bed on top of me they'd better paralyze me or something, or I'll—"

"Here," Jandik interrupted, raising his lantern.

Regdar looked up and saw deep furrows scratched into the top of the cylindrical tunnel—the murderer's trail.

"Well done," Regdar said to the tracker. "Lead on."

Considering the many setbacks of the previous night, his lack of sleep, and a dreary turn in the weather, Vargussel felt sure he radiated an aura of confidence as he strode into the duke's private office for the second time in as many days. Even after making arrangements to secure the slaughterhouse, he had at least had the opportunity to go home, clean himself up a bit, and change before he received the duke's summons. A trail of cologne wafted behind him, and his clean, crisp robe rustled as he walked.

Vargussel bowed deeply to the duke and said, "Your Highness, I attend you at your request."

The duke, who was seated behind his desk, motioned to a chair and watched with an appraising eye as Vargussel sat.

"You're well?" the duke asked.

Vargussel sighed inwardly, finding no patience left for the duke's imbecilic questions.

"I am most fit, Your Highness," he answered. "Again, I find myself deep in study and experimentation. I understand that His Highness is a busy man as well, so please do not allow a few scrapes and bumps to distract you from the matter at hand, a matter I am sure is one of utmost urgency and with dire consequences for us all."

The duke smiled, and Vargussel returned the expression. His groveling before his master's image had left Vargussel with the odd scrape, cut, and bruise, but what little pain there had been had turned to an irritating itch. That didn't do much for Vargussel's patience.

Vargussel again suppressed a sigh—this time of relief—when the duke reached into a drawer and didn't ask after his health again.

"Lord Constable Regdar has found something," the duke said.

Vargussel tipped an eyebrow up, not having to feign interest in the progress of the new lord constable.

The duke set something hard and heavy down on the desk in front of Vargussel. When his hand came away from it, Vargussel let slip a slight gasp at the sight of a jagged chunk of his shield guardian's armor.

"Did he see what this came from?" Vargussel asked.

"You recognize it?"

Vargussel stopped himself before he answered. Instead, he shook his head and reached for the piece of metal.

"May I?" the wizard asked.

The duke nodded and said, "Be my guest."

The piece of armor wasn't big and hadn't obviously effected the shield guardian's functioning, but a piece of the construct in the duke's possession could be troublesome for Vargussel. If the duke summoned a wizard to—

"You want me to tell you what it is," Vargussel said, holding back a relieved giggle.

"I do," the duke replied. "The lord constable didn't get a clear look at the thing but he managed to slice a chunk out of it. Looks like armorer's steel to me, but we need to know more. I'm told there's a spell . . . ?"

"Legend lore," the wizard said.

"That's the one," replied the duke. "Can you do it?"

"Indeed I can, Your Highness. Indeed I can."

"The duchy will, of course, reimburse you for your trouble," the duke said.

Vargussel smiled and let the piece of his own construct roll around in his palm.

"Please, Your Highness," he said. "I am a loyal subject of the duchy and her duke. It would only be my pleasure and honor to cast a spell for you, that we might bring these heinous acts of senseless murder to a close."

"Very well," said the duke. "The duchy thanks you. Now. . . ."

"Ah, yes," Vargussel said, "with all due haste. I can cast the spell at once if that meets with your approval. There isn't much to it but some muttering and waving about of hands. A picture will form in my mind, and I will know the origin of this steel."

The duke nodded, and Vargussel held the piece of metal out in front of him.

Legend lore, indeed, the wizard thought.

He began to speak a string of nonsense that he made up as he went along but which he was sure the duke would mistake for the language of magic. The spell he actually intended to cast could be done in seconds, but when one is performing for royalty, best make a show of it. After a suitable period of time mumbling nonsense and wiggling his fingers over the steel, Vargussel uttered the real words of power and twisted his fingers just so.

A faint, blue glow sprang from his palm, lighting the steel from below.

The duke sat forward, peering at the effect with undisguised awe. It was all Vargussel could do not to laugh at him. The glow was a meaningless prestidigitation, a parlor trick for the amusement of children. It told Vargussel nothing and would tell the duke no more.

He let the glow persist until the duke was solidly at the edge of his seat, then he pretended to see something in the air between them. The duke followed his eyes, of course seeing nothing, but seemed to fully believe that Vargussel was reading something written in eldritch script in the very air itself.

When he thought he'd laid it on thick enough, Vargussel let the glow fade away, and he curled his fingers around the piece of his shield guardian.

"Alas," he said, taking care to add a tone of dire seriousness to his voice, "our opponent is powerful indeed."

"What did you see?" asked the duke.

Vargussel shook his head and narrowed his eyes.

"Vargussel," the duke prodded. "Speak, for the love of—"

"It is warded," the wizard said.

"Warded?" asked the duke.

"Protected," Vargussel said. "This comes from a most capable spellcaster, I can assure you, Your Highness. It has been made proof against spells such as the one I cast upon it. It is as if a wall of shadow has descended over its history and its maker."

The duke sighed and all but sagged back into his chair.

"But all is not lost, Your Highness," Vargussel said.

"There's another spell?"

"There is always another spell, sire," said the wizard. "I will need time, though, and resources from my laboratory."

"How long?"

"A day," Vargussel lied, "perhaps longer. The magic is powerful and carefully masked."

The duke nodded, looking down at nothing, thinking.

"May I take it with me?" the wizard prompted.

"You had best," answered the duke. "Keep it in your sight at all times, though."

"I will," Vargussel agreed.

"A day, you said?" asked the duke.

"Perhaps more," the wizard answered.

The duke frowned and said, "Do your best to tell me something sooner. The lives of a score of city watchmen and Lord Constable Regdar may depend on it."

"Indeed?" Vargussel asked, feigning surprise.

"They pursue the creature from which this steel was severed even now," the duke said, his face lined and gray.

"Do they?" Vargussel murmured. "Do they indeed. . . ."

Naull didn't know how long they'd been in the sewers before she finally figured out a way to breathe through her mouth that actually cut the force of the stench. The air had a thickness to it that made it coat everything it touched with the smell of waste and decay.

The tunnel was the same size all the way in, but it still seemed to be closing in on her a little tighter with every step she took. They kept a steady pace and turned only a few times as they delved deeper into the city's eastern reaches: the sprawling and crowded Trade Quarter. To Naull it felt like they'd been wading through sewage for miles but the city wasn't that big. She thought she might be able to clear her head and start thinking straight if only she could take a deep breath. Instead, she tensed her whole body, riding waves of trembling panic while remaining stoic and silent on the outside.

"Here," Jandik said from the head of the single-file line. He pointed to the low ceiling, and Regdar stepped up to follow the tracker's finger as it drew a line from just over his head, down the tunnel into the impenetrable darkness. "This is where the scratches stop. We kept going about another hundred yards without seeing another sign. It's as if the thing just disappeared."

Regdar looked around, and so did everyone else. The walls and ceiling of the tunnel were made of old but solid brickwork. There was no sign of a door and certainly no visible magical effects.

"It could be under our feet," Watch Sergeant Lorec suggested.

Regdar seemed to consider the idea, even scuffled his toes around under the opaque, brown liquid, feeling for a door or hinge. If there was a trapdoor in the floor of the tunnel, opening it would have sent thousands of gallons of water emptying into the space below.

"I don't think so," he said. "The thing that attacked us was made of steel or encased in steel armor. If it had been submerged, the piece I cut off would have been wet, or at least stained with this horrid soup. It was clean and dry."

"There's another secret door," Naull suggested. "There has to be."

"Can you cast that spell again?" asked Regdar.

Naull smiled and said, "That's what I'm here for, isn't it?"

Regdar looked at her strangely and shrugged.

She closed her eyes and did her best to ignore him, the walls and the stench still closing in on her, along with the feeling of impending doom that she couldn't for the life of her shake. Naull cast her spell. She heard Watchman Samoth slosh a few steps away from her as she intoned the incantation, but ignored that too.

When the spell was done, she opened her eyes and was greeted by a dazzling, green glow from the wall to the party's left. She stepped to the wall and traced the outline of the door with her fingertip. Regdar leaned in close.

"I see it," he whispered.

"Can she open it?" the sergeant asked.

Naull kept her focus on the spell, digging deep into her magic-enhanced awareness for the door's hidden latch.

"Can she?" the sergeant pressed.

Regdar shushed him, and Naull silently applauded his patience. It took a minute more than she thought it would, but eventually her eyes locked on a chip of mortar at the edge of the door. She clearly saw her hand extend toward it and tip the mortar chip down as if picking it out of the wall. The door swung wide, revealing—

Naull shook her head, wiping the spell away, with her hand still poised an inch from the trigger. With the magic gone, she couldn't see the door.

"Is that the latch?" Regdar asked.

She thought about opening it to show off her cleverness but quickly reminded herself what might be behind the door. She swallowed and found her throat dry and painful.

"Just, um . . ." she said. "Just scratch it like you're trying to pull it out, and the door will swing inward."

Regdar gave her a smile that she tried to return, then he turned to the tracker.

"I'll take point from here," the lord constable said.

Jandik didn't argue. None of them did.

Vargussel threw open the door to his study and went immediately to the apothecary's cabinet in which he stored his spell components. He opened just the four drawers he needed and quickly gathered up the components of the spell. Heedless of whatever papers might have been on his desk, he ran through the spell as quickly as possible, mixing the noxious components in a sizzling, smoking paste that almost caused a sheet of parchment to catch flame.

The mixture was gone in a puff of smoke, and Vargussel finished the spell. He closed his eyes and formed in his imagination a picture of the lord constable's face. It took no more than a few heartbeats but Vargussel found his heart racing and his fingers tapping with impatience as the image formed more clearly, then took life in his mind.

Regdar was in the sewers. Vargussel could see him as clearly as if they were standing toe-to-toe, though in truth they were separated by a mile or more.

Stairs, the lord constable said, his voice echoing in Vargussel's mind, somehow disconnected by magic, time, and distance from the image of his lips forming the words.

Vargussel hissed out a curse. They were at the sewer stairs. They had found the second of his secret doors. They would be in the slaughterhouse soon enough.

The wizard watched and listened as Regdar mustered his pitiful force of impotent city watchmen and some girl Vargussel had never seen. They started up the stairs.

I had time, Lord Constable, Vargussel thought. I was ready for you. You'll see just how ready soon enough.

As Regdar and his people ascended the stairs, Vargussel fingered his amulet, watching, waiting patiently.

Regdar fought the urge to crouch the whole time he moved up the stairs. The ceiling was tall enough so that he could stand up straight, but just barely. The stairs were wider than he'd have expected, though. The telltale scratches ran all the way up the ceiling and lined both walls. Whatever it was they were tracking had definitely gone that way, back and forth maybe dozens of times.

The stairs looped back over themselves and stopped at a wider space, like a vestibule or foyer. Straight ahead of them was a heavy oak door bound with iron bands. Regdar stopped, waiting for the others to gather, though only Lorec and Jandik could fit in the space behind him. He couldn't even see Naull.

"I make it about sixty feet up from the sewer tunnel," Regdar said.

Lorec shrugged, and Jandik nodded.

"We should be about ten or fifteen feet below the surface, if I guess right," the tracker said.

"Basement depth?" asked Lorec.

Regdar shrugged and turned to examine the door. There was no obvious lock, just a big, heavy, iron ring.

"Why am I getting a bad feeling about this door?" Regdar asked no one in particular.

"Because you're not an idiot," Sergeant Lorec answered, then seemed to remember himself. "I mean, because you have good instincts, Lord Constable."

Regdar waved off the young man's embarrassment and briefly pined for Lidda. She could have examined the door for traps, removed them, then picked the lock. Regdar sighed at the thought that what he needed right then was a thief, but he was surrounded by the watch.

"I'll open it, milord," Lorec said, squaring his shoulders.

Regdar smiled, held his shield up to cover his face, and said, "I've got it, Sergeant, but thank you."

Reaching around his shield, Regdar tugged at the iron ring, but the door held fast. Nothing shot, squirted, exploded, or hissed out at him, and he didn't drop dead or burst into flames, so Regdar had to assume it was just locked.

"Stand back," he said.

The two men pushed back to the top of the stairs, the others giving way behind them.

Regdar whirled and kicked the door hard just below the iron ring. The blow sent a resounding thud echoing down the stairs and tendrils of electric pain tingling up Regdar's leg. The door didn't budge.

"You hit that hard, milord," Lorec said. "It damn well should have opened."

Regdar rubbed his leg and called for Naull.

By the time she made her way up the stairs through the others, Regdar's leg was beginning to feel normal again.

"I've heard there are spells to keep a door closed," he said.

Naull looked at the door, took a long, deep breath in the stale but not odorous air, and said, "One or two. I had a feeling we'd be in a position like this, breaking into a murderer's secret hideaway and all."

She stared at the door and whispered a string of nonsense words. It seemed to Regdar that they should have echoed more in the confined space. Once spoken, the words fell dead as if they had weight.

There was a click, then a creak, and the door eased open a few inches.

Regdar put out a hand to push past Naull, startling her.

"Jandik," he said, "bring that light up."

The tracker came forward and Regdar carefully drew his greatsword. He stepped through the door into a wide room made from mortared flagstones. There was another iron-bound oak door in the wall to his right and a third across the room. A single sheet of parchment was nailed to the door on the other side of the room. Regdar could just barely make out what looked like writing from across the dimly lit room. Otherwise the space was empty and seemed not to have been used in some time.

Jandik stepped in next to Regdar and they both examined the floor. Thick dust was everywhere but there were obvious tracks—furrows almost—connecting all three doors.

"Looks like either one," Jandik said, "or both."

As the others filed into the room, Regdar said, "Sergeant Lorec, take Jandik, Asil, and Samoth, and go through that way." He pointed at the door with the parchment nailed to it and Lorec started crossing the room immediately. "Naull, Lem, and Drahir will come with me this way. Bring me that parchment first, though," he added.

Lorec was already there. Regdar saw him reach for the parchment while leaning in to read it from Samoth's lanternlight.

The sergeant's hand never made it to the parchment before it was blown off in a blast of air, fire, wood, iron, dust, blood, and shattered bone.

Regdar was pushed back and fell sprawling against the wall, only dimly aware of pain and heat, screams and grunts.

"Damn you," Vargussel muttered to Regdar, though the lord constable couldn't hear him. "Have you no intellectual curiosity at all?"

The explosive runes were meant for Regdar, but who knew the lord constable would send some lowly watch sergeant to read it?

Though it was hard for Vargussel to see through the clouds of dust and smoke filling the room, he could see Regdar scramble to his feet, virtually unharmed. The young woman was coughing, waving away the smoke, but also still standing. One of the watchmen at least seemed to have survived, and he ran out of the room, coughing and gagging.

The smoke continued billowing and Vargussel could just make out the shape of a man laying on the floor, his skin and clothing ablaze.

Vargussel smiled at the fact that he'd hurt them at least—maybe enough to turn back their little expedition into his private affairs. He stopped smiling when he heard the woman begin casting a spell.

She ran through it well, managing not to cough, and Vargussel cursed her the whole way.

What will it be? he thought. A gust of wind, a wind wall ... something to blow away the smoke?"

The room filled with pelting, fast-driving sleet. The dull crystals were driven by a strong wind, falling almost sideways in the confined space. The few watchmen that still stood scurried around in a panic as the woman tried to assure them that it was "all right" and that they shouldn't panic.

"Sleet storm," Vargussel whispered, then thought: This one has a flair for the dramatic.

It didn't take long for the conjured storm to clear the room of smoke, drive the dampened dust to the floor, and put out the fires.

Vargussel shrugged. At least he could see better.

The runes did their work well. The sergeant was dead. His right hand was gone completely and his face was a blackened, ruined mass of scorched flesh. The watchman who held the lantern for his sergeant had been thrown back a good eight feet and lay crumpled on the floor in a position only someone with a broken back could accomplish.

One of the others seemed to have stabbed himself through the thigh with his own sword. He sat against a wall, twitching, shivering in a pool of freezing sleet, bleeding.

Jandik, Regdar called to the man as he slipped across the floor to him. *It's all right. You're going to be all right.*

That made Vargussel laugh.

"Don't let me . . ." Jandik gasped, blood foaming on his quivering lips, his eyes rolling up to lazily scan Regdar's face. "Don't let me . . . die here. It stinks."

Regdar forced himself to laugh and got a smile from the wounded tracker. He was rifling through his pack, crouching over the fallen watchman.

"You're not going to die here," Regdar reassured the man. "You're under my command, and I don't remember giving you any such order."

"Lorec . . ." Jandik coughed out, "and Samoth . . ."

Regdar's fingers found the vial he was looking for and pulled it out of his pack with a jerk.

"I'll deal with them myself," Regdar joked darkly as he peeled the wax off the cork. "Now, I want you to drink this . . . all of it."

"No . . ." the tracker mumbled halfheartedly, wiping sleet, blood, and dust from his hair. "Don't waste that on—"

Regdar pushed the vial past the tracker's lips and smiled again as Jandik greedily drank the contents of the vial. When it was empty, Regdar gently drew it away from Jandik's mouth. The tracker leaned forward, trying to suck any last drop from the vial.

"Easy," Regdar said, "you got it all. It should just take a—"

He stopped when he heard something he thought was an armored footstep echo quietly from the dark space behind the ruined door.

"Did you hear that?" Naull whispered as Regdar stood.

Jandik coughed, wiped his lips on the back of a hand, and coughed again. The second time, no blood came with it. The tracker took a deep breath.

Regdar put up a hand for silence and the group of survivors obeyed. As he waited for the sound to come again, Regdar scanned the corpse of Watch Sergeant Lorec, doing his best to see the ruined body of one of his men in terms of resources rather than emotion. His eyes settled on the sergeant's sword just when the sound came again. There was no mistaking it that time.

Regdar held his greatsword in one hand as he bent to retrieve the dead sergeant's shining, polished long sword. It was probably an heirloom, and Regdar quickly, silently promised himself to return it to the sergeant's family, but he had use of it first.

"Something's moving in there," Regdar whispered to the others, who had gathered behind him.

He flipped the long sword over in his grip and held it out, pommel-first, to Lem, the next in line among the watchmen. Lem took the sword, admiring its gleaming blade.

"I can't take this," Lem whispered. "This is magical, or I'm a son of a naga."

"Shut up and use it," Regdar replied, putting both hands on his own greatsword. "Stay right behind me. Whatever is in there, I want you to kill it. Understood?"

Lem nodded, then exchanged a worried glance with Asil and Drahir.

"Drahir," Regdar continued, "get up here with that lantern. Stand just behind Lem. Naull, I need you behind Drahir. Asil, stay back with Jandik and keep an eye on our exit."

"I'm fine," the tracker said as he staggered to his feet, leaning against the wall and wincing with pain. "That potion did the trick."

Regdar was about to protest when the sound of a pile of rocks shifting—it could only be that—echoed from the space behind the door. He knew the time for planning and talking was over, and he stepped across the threshold into darkness.

"Go on, fools," Vargussel murmured to the image in his mind. "Let the little one serve some function after all."

The parchment and the spell cast on it had been a ruse—simple but effective. It hadn't managed to kill Regdar but it was succeeding in its second mission: drawing intruders down the wrong path.

Vargussel watched Regdar slip into the shadows. The mage rubbed his hands together nervously in anticipation of the moment when—

The lord constable sank into a fighting stance and called out, *Engaged!*—whatever that meant.

The dread guard stepped up over a pile of rubble—stone, bricks, and wood piled three feet high—where one of the walls had collapsed, decades gone by. Regdar stood in a corridor that ran the length of the west end of the slaughterhouse's basement. To the lord constable's right was the ruin of two rooms that once served as storage but had come to be the watchpost of Vargussel's earlier effort in the creation of a magical construct.

The dread guard had cost Vargussel dearly at the time, but it proved too stupid, too slow, and too weak for his greater purposes. It could never wield the death ray but it could pick off unwary intruders.

Regdar easily deflected the dread guard's first attack but the construct fought on. It had no other choice, no survival instinct, no independent mind.

Vargussel sat back and watched.

Naull could see the man who attacked Regdar but couldn't see his face. He was wearing a rusted but once grand suit of banded armor and an elaborately plumed helm with a visor that covered the whole of his face. The broadsword with which he deftly parried Regdar's bigger blade was undoubtedly enchanted.

The man was shorter than Regdar by a hand or more, and though the armor was heavy, Naull couldn't imagine the dark, rusted knight making the booming footsteps Regdar and other witnesses had described. Still, she'd learned not to judge a book by its cover, and she knew well enough that though he looked like a normal man, he could still be strong enough to flip over the bed. The holes in the floor had been carved with magic, and the young aristocrats had been killed magically as well.

Naull brought to mind a simple spell that she hoped might end things quickly. In the cramped, tumbledown space, Regdar was slashing at the knight with his greatsword, keeping Lem and the others back. Jandik looked like he was itching to fight but his wounds were still too painful, and he had trouble just keeping on his feet. From the others Naull could sense the same palpable feeling of relief that she was experiencing herself. They'd found their murderer and he was a man in armor, not a monster, not a godlike steel demon from some sewer-reeking hell.

Naull cast the spell, focusing all of its energy at the dark knight. She fully expected him to crumple to the rubble-strewn floor at Regdar's feet, fast asleep, but the armored warrior didn't oblige. To Naull it seemed as if the spell had passed right through the strange man as if he wasn't even there.

There could be any number of reasons for that, she told herself, but still....

She felt that sense of relief and hope quickly fading back to anxiety and panic.

Regdar banged another of the strange knight's attacks away while stepping back and to the left. He'd taken the measure of his opponent and found the dark knight strong and insistent, brave and relentless—but slow and predictable. He expected the knight to slash high at his throat with a cross-chest backhand, and that's just what the mysterious man did.

Rather than wave his own sword in front of himself to parry the slash, Regdar crouched and let the blow pass just over the top of his head. The dark knight was momentarily unbalanced with most of his weight on his right foot and his left foot almost off the floor.

Regdar let himself fall back on his rear as he kicked out with his right foot, slamming it hard into the inside of the dark knight's right knee.

The stranger's right knee emitted a loud snap and collapsed, sending him sprawling in a clatter of steel onto the top of the rubble pile. Regdar was surprised that the man didn't grunt, cry out, or make any sound at all either when his knee was dislocated or when he fell facefirst onto a pile of sharp stones and splintered wood. The dark knight's helmet popped loose when his neck snapped at the end of the fall and before Regdar could spin up to his feet, the knight was already standing, even though he was missing a head.

The helm rolled off the pile of rubble and came to rest against Regdar's foot but it was empty. In front of Regdar stood the knight, his weight on his undamaged left leg, his sword swinging into a guard position, and just an empty space where his head should have been.

It was no man, Regdar realized, but a suit of armor come independently to life.

The armor hacked down with its broadsword and Regdar bashed the blade away so hard the broadsword whirled out of the animated gauntlet and clattered against the ceiling before sliding to a stop behind the pile of rubble.

The animated armor turned at the shoulders, as if it still had eyes or even a head to house them, and looked for its sword. Regdar chopped into its pauldron. The force of the blow drove the armor suit down to the rubble.

It reached out a hand for Regdar's throat but the lord constable jerked back, freeing his sword from the twisted metal of the thing's shoulder, then punched through with the point of his greatsword into the thing's breastplate. The wide, heavy blade sank into the space where the dark knight's heart should have been, and the armor twitched in response, then fell still.

Regdar withdrew his blade with a tooth-rattling shriek of steel on steel and stood ready for several heartbeats until he was satisfied that the thing wasn't going to get back up.

"Drahir," Regdar called back over his shoulder, "take its sword."

Vargussel was beginning to get nervous. The intruders had dealt with the dread guard too easily. He'd hoped it would kill at least one of the watchmen but Regdar hadn't even given them a chance to fight. The young mage had wasted a spell on it, at least, and Vargussel could take that as a minor victory, but overall the construct that had cost him forty thousand gold Merchants had hardly even frightened them.

"Think you killed it, Lord Constable," Vargussel hoped aloud. "Think that's what came for you in your bedchamber."

If Regdar was stupid enough to think that the dread guard was the assassin they were looking for, they might take their wounded and their assumed victory and go home.

This wasn't it, Regdar said to his men.

Vargussel hissed out an exasperated sigh.

"You may be suffering from late-onset intelligence, Lord Constable," he said to the image of Regdar, "but you've a long way to go before you get to me, and I've been smarter than you for a long time."

Grinding his teeth, Vargussel watched in silence as one of the watchmen retrieved the broadsword that alone had cost him nearly nine thousand Merchants. Regdar gathered his party around him, leaving his two wounded men in the anteroom, and pressed on.

The mage watched as they explored the ruined wing of the basement. They found the stairs leading up to the ground floor that had caved in and been blocked for decades. He watched them run through their elaborate rituals of listening, touching, feeling, thinking, and pondering at the first of two intact doors. Finally Regdar just kicked it in and Vargussel had to tap his fingers waiting for them to satisfy themselves that the room beyond was indeed empty.

They did the same for the second door, and Vargussel found himself yawning. They found the old stairs behind the second door blocked by another cave-in. They wouldn't get down to the killing floor that way.

"You'll have to come in the front door," the mage whispered, "just as planned."

Vargussel briefly wished for the confidence to laugh maniacally but instead he just set his chin on his hands and watched.

They regrouped in the anteroom, all eyes on Regdar, and Naull took a deep breath.

"What we encountered in the inn," Regdar said, "and what was described by witnesses was much bigger, much stronger than that suit of ghost armor."

"Dread guard," Naull said.

Regdar looked at her and she felt herself blush but didn't know why.

"It's a magical construct," she said. "Powerful mages use them as guards."

" 'Powerful' mages?" said Jandik, who could stand without leaning on the wall, though he still kept one hand pressed to his bruised midsection. "How powerful?"

Naull shrugged and said, "I'm not sure how to answer that. Its not as if there's a scale that assigns someone a number so you can immediately know the extent of his abilities."

"On a scale of one to ten," Regdar offered with a wink.

Naull shrugged again, and said, "Fifteen?"

The watchmen visibly sagged.

"Great," Asil whispered. "That's just great."

"You think someone's building these things and sending them out to kill people?" Regdar asked.

Naull shrugged a third time and said, "I have no idea. All we can know for certain is that the dread guard was built by someone and left in there with instructions to attack. The parchment with the explosive runes was put on the door by an equally skilled wizard. I don't know how long they sat there, but now that we're here, it seems they weren't guarding much of anything."

"And the dread guard, as you call it," Regdar added, "is smaller than what we're looking for."

Jandik took a deep breath and said, "It was a decoy."

Regdar nodded. Lem, Asil, and Drahir each took a step back. If Naull didn't know any better, she thought it looked like they were ready to run. She realized then that she didn't actually know better and they might be.

"There's only one other way out," Jandik continued.

All eyes were drawn to the door Naull and Regdar had been about to open when the parchment exploded.

Regdar, his greatsword still in his left hand, strode to the door in question and stopped within arm's reach of it. He glanced back and Jandik limped forward, holding a lantern. Lem and Drahir followed with their new magic swords, if a bit reluctantly. Asil staggered to Jandik's side and they ended up leaning on each other.

Naull ran through the spells she still had at her command. As if on cue Regdar asked, "Can you open this door like you did the one from the stairs?"

She had cast that spell and would need time before being able to cast it again.

"No," she said. "If it's locked the same way, you'll have to break it down."

"Anything on the other side," Jandik warned, "will know we're coming."

"There was an explosion in here that killed two men," Lem said.

"Yeah," Drahir added, "and some kind of snow storm."

"It was rain," Asil corrected.

"Actually," Naull said, "it was sleet."

The watchmen nodded and Regdar sighed.

"Whatever's behind that door," the lord constable said, "already knows we're here."

Everyone but Regdar went pale.

Regdar, greatsword still in one hand, kicked the door and kicked it hard. It didn't open but Naull heard the wood crack at least a little. She knew enough about the magic that was likely holding the door closed to realize that it would be hard, but Regdar could eventually kick it in.

The lord constable sighed and gave the door a second kick. Jandik held up his lantern in a hand shaking from fear, pain, and loss of blood. The effect was a flickering light that sent shadows twitching across the walls. Naull's hair stood on end. Lem and Drahir held their swords up and ready, their own shaking hands sending flashes of reflected light flickering across their enchanted blades.

Regdar kicked the door again, and there was a louder crack. One side of the door was bent outward, the wood cracking around the iron bands.

One more kick and the door broke inward with an echoing crash. Regdar shifted his greatsword into a two-hand grip and swung the blade over his head as he stepped boldly through the door.

Naull closed her eyes, tense, waiting for the sound of steel on steel or of another explosion, or the roar of some fell beast, but none of those things came.

"Come in behind me and watch your step," Regdar said. "There's something strange in here."

Vargussel absentmindedly rolled a piece of parchment between his fingers until he'd made a long, thin tube of it.

They're in, he thought.

His mind descended into a flurry of unspoken curses, many of which he was embarrassed for even thinking.

They had broken through the door into the slaughterhouse and were steps from his laboratory. What was worse, the damnable woman had set them thinking along a course that brought them closer to the truth than they knew. Yes, someone had built the dread guard, and yes it was a decoy, and yes whoever it was was a powerful wizard, and yes that powerful wizard had built it with the express purpose of killing certain young suitors for the hand of fair Maelani. That last bit might have been a piece of the puzzle still missing for them but still they were farther along than Vargussel would have liked.

Regdar stepped through the door ready for anything but there was nothing there yet. He stood on a wooden platform twenty feet above the killing floor. The platform was built against the southwest wall of the huge room, and there was a flight of wooden stairs that emptied onto the killing floor itself.

Regdar couldn't see the stairs and neither could Vargussel. The steps were cloaked in a thick, roiling gray mist—a fog of Vargussel's own creation.

The mage watched Regdar scan the room. He saw the lord constable's eyes linger on the twisting fences that once led streams of cattle to their doom. He saw his rival's eyes trace the path of the steel tracks on the ceiling from which dangled chains on the ends of which were rusty meat hooks, their grisly loads long since gone.

The far side of the large space was shrouded in gray fog that reached halfway up the high walls and was placed just so to conceal

Vargussel's laboratory along with his mightiest creation.

Come in behind me and watch your step, Regdar said to his charges. *There's something strange in here.*

The others wandered in behind him, and Vargussel was pleased to see the masks of fear on all their faces. The wounded tracker was having difficulty walking despite Regdar's healing potion and was relegated to holding a lantern. The other wounded watchman stood arm-in-arm with the tracker, and they helped each other along.

They were the first to follow Regdar onto the platform, and Vargussel sat up, holding his breath in anticipation. The wounded tracker spotted the low railing on the north end of the platform and steered his companion toward it, obviously hoping to rest their weight against it. They made it two steps before the whole north half of the platform gave way.

Vargussel laughed, and when he clapped his hands, the rolled bit of parchment he'd been fiddling with wafted to the floor. The wounded men fell in a cloud of dust and rotten wood, twenty feet to the killing floor. Regdar backed up a step, regaining his own balance and leaning up against the south wall. The young woman poked her head through the door and said, *What happened?*

The floor collapsed, Regdar told her.

The exchange demonstrated everything Vargussel thought was wrong with the fools. *Obviously* the floor had collapsed.

The lord constable looked in the direction of the stairs, eyeing the fog with reasonable suspicion.

Looks like stairs over here, he said to the woman, again mastering the obvious.

I don't like that fog at all, one of the watchmen said from the safety of the anteroom.

Regdar looked at the stairs again and stepped away from the wall.

Neither do I, the lord constable said, but he went to the top of the stairs anyway and stepped into the fog.

"Go ahead," Vargussel whispered, placing the palm of his right hand over the amulet that controlled the shield guardian.

The mage sent a portion of his thoughts into the amulet, through the link, and to the construct.

Now, he sent. *They come.*

Naull stepped through the door and was startled when someone grabbed her arm from behind. She turned and Lem smiled at her, then glanced at the ruined platform. She smiled back, nodded, and stepped onto the wooden planks. The half of the platform that was against the south wall of the slaughterhouse had held Regdar's considerably greater weight well enough but Naull was still hesitant about it. Heights had never been her strong suit.

With Lem still holding her arm, ready to snatch her back into the anteroom should the rest of the platform give way, Naull stepped farther out—far enough to peer over the jagged edge, down to where the two watchmen had fallen.

She could see one of them, partially buried in the broken planks, a cloud of dust settling around him. It looked to be Asil, and he wasn't moving. Lying facedown as he was, she couldn't see his face.

Naull looked over at Regdar, who was waist deep in roiling gray fog, and she swallowed in a dry throat.

"Are they all right?" he asked from over his shoulder, pausing for a reply.

Naull shook her head and answered, "I can't tell. Asil isn't moving. I can't hear anything."

She looked back down and enough of the dust had settled that she could see Jandik, or at least the bottom half of him. The rest was buried under broken planks of rotten wood. He wasn't moving either.

She turned to tell Regdar and was just in time to see the top of his helmed head sink silently into the obscuring mist. Her breath caught in her throat.

She stepped away from the door, crossing halfway to the stairs, having slipped out of Lem's gentle hold. She stopped, looked back at the door, and saw Lem and Samoth follow her out and peer over the edge themselves.

"Constable Jandik!" Lem called. "Asil . . . are you all right?"

They all waited for the space of a few quick breaths but there was no answer.

Naull looked out over the room and the sight of the fog made her shiver. It was obviously conjured in some way. The edges were too straight, almost at right angles. The fog was meant to hide something. It extended as high as the floor of the platform, and obscured about a quarter of the huge space that was the abandoned killing floor. It didn't drift like natural fog, but seemed almost contained by glass walls or some other, invisible force.

The platform trembled and Naull heard a low thud as if something heavy had fallen to the ground. She pressed herself against the wall, and Lem did the same. Samoth ducked back into the anteroom.

"What was that?" Samoth asked.

Both he and Lem looked at Naull, who said, "It's the . . . thing." She turned to face the stairs and shouted, "Regdar!"

There was no answer.

"Regdar!" she called again, louder than before.

She jumped when a hand touched her arm. It was Lem again.

"He won't answer," the watchman said. "He won't want to give away his position in that pea soup."

"Lem!" Samoth hissed from the doorway. "Get over here ... Jandik's lantern."

"Damn," Lem breathed, skipping across the ruined platform to Samoth's side. The two of them looked down. "Jandik was holding a lantern when they fell. The flame's caught on all that old wood."

Another low, booming thud vibrated the platform, and Naull said, "They'll burn alive."

"If they aren't dead already," Samoth mumbled.

"We have to climb down there," Lem said, already slipping out of his canvas rucksack.

"Wait," Naull said. "Regdar's—"

"Got enough trouble," Lem interrupted, "with whatever's making that booming sound."

Naull nodded and looked out over the magic fog as Lem and Samoth gathered up their lengths of rope and tied them to anything that looked strong enough to hold.

The sound came again, closer.

Naull ran through what spells she had left but she'd have to see the thing to use them.

The sound came again, much closer, and Lem started climbing down.

Regdar judged his arms to be about two and a half feet long, and he knew the blade of his greatsword was five and half feet in length. He held the blade straight out in front of him and couldn't see the tip.

Five feet, he guessed, no more.

He stood at the foot of the stairs on a damp, rough, stone floor, surrounded by gray fog as featureless and unyielding as endless Limbo itself. He could hear the thing approaching and could hear the voices of his comrades. He was happy they weren't following him. Naull's spells would be as dangerous to friends in the fog as to enemies, and Lem and Samoth were better off climbing down to save their fellows from the fire.

Lord Constable. . . .

Regdar repeated the words in his mind. It was up to him.

The floor trembled under another booming footstep, and Regdar held his greatsword in a ready stance that protected his head and the front of his body. He might only be able to see five feet ahead of him but that was all the room he needed.

Another footstep, and the thing was close—very close.

As the vibration subsided, Regdar heard a boot scrape the rough floor next to him. He turned slowly, keeping ready to defend himself. He could see the vague outline of a man against the gray nothing of the fog.

"Lord Constable," Lem whispered, "it's me . . . Lem."

Regdar would have nodded but wasn't sure Lem could see him.

"Stay there," the lord constable whispered.

"I'm outside the fog," the watchman whispered back. "I can just barely see you."

Another booming footstep, and Regdar could tell that it was very, very close. He turned and saw a shadow looming up in the mist. It had the shape of a man but the behemoth was easily eight feet tall. Without a second's hesitation, Regdar charged, bringing his sword around in a high, hard slash aimed at the thing's midsection. He'd moved only half a step when the shadow thrust out its left hand and Regdar's mind registered a flash of light.

His body moved faster than his conscious mind. Regdar let the momentum of his sword slash spin his body down and under the streak of ragged, yellow lightning that burst from the shadow's outstretched palm. The lightning bolt passed within an inch of Regdar's face, and he had the unpleasant feeling of each tiny whisker standing on end, as if drawn to the bolt. The mist turned instantly to nearly boiling water that scalded his face but he managed to dodge it.

Regdar's spin brought his face around to see the lightning bolt slam the shadowy form of Lem full in the chest. The watchman never had a chance. Caught in the lightning's deadly embrace, Lem shook on his feet as if dangling from wires, his whole body convulsing. The mist was blasted away and Regdar saw the watchman's eyes burst in a shower of pink fluid. He smelled Lem's flesh burning a moment before the bolt bounced back, arcing angrily from Lem to Regdar.

The lord constable wasn't as fast or as lucky the second time. The bolt hit him in the right thigh. His armor seemed suddenly made of a million stinging bees and his eyes, jaw, and other orifices clamped tightly shut. He could hear himself rattle out a staccato groan, then it was gone as fast as it hit him.

He opened his eyes, waiting for the lightning to hit him again.

Naull watched Lem's twitching body fall to the floor, heard Regdar groan, and didn't have time to scream before an arc of blinding yellow light spat out of the fog and touched Samoth in the chest. The watchman blew out his breath in a stuttering moan and flapped his arms at his sides as if he was trying to take wing. All that happened in less than a second, then the lightning bounced off him and back into the mist.

There was a sound like a sack of rice being dropped on the floor, then the sound of wood exploding—she'd heard enough of that lately that the sound would never leave her.

Before she could think of what might have been broken, the chain lightning arced again, finding Asil's steel armor. The fallen watchman twitched as if he was being pummeled by the jagged bolt but he made no sound. From there the lightning bolt shot at Samoth again. The watchman had survived the first blow, if just barely, and was on his knees, holding his face in his hands. The lightning took him in the back and though it looked like it should have pushed him forward, Samoth jerked backward so hard and so fast that Naull heard something snap in the suffering watchman. Samoth's limp form fell as the lightning traced a vision-smearing arc straight upward, clawing at one of the dangling meat hooks and creating a puff of burning, powdered rust in the air. It snaked to a second hook, and Naull watched it with paralyzed fascination.

The bolt touched another hook startlingly close to the edge of the platform. Naull bent her knees, ready to jump.

The next bounce took the lightning bolt down at such an odd angle it seemed almost to curve around the edge of the wooden platform. It hit something, and Naull heard Regdar grunt loudly, then say, "Damn it!"

Finally she took a breath, relieved that he was at least alive, and she only dimly registered the lightning bolt arcing to another meat hook, then straight at her. If she ever thought she might be able to dodge that, she must have been mad.

The bolt struck her left earring and rattled her head. Every hair on her body stood on end and she could swear she felt the fluid in her eyes start to boil. She couldn't see and hoped it was because her eyes were closed, not because they'd burst in her skull.

Her eyes snapped open and she saw the lightning bolt tracing a line from her to another meat hook, then it released her and she fell to her knees riding a wave of excruciating pain.

Naull fell onto her stomach, coughing as she tried to get her lungs to work in rhythm again. From that vantage point she could see the lightning jiggle poor, dead Samoth again, and she was sure the bolt was thinner, dimmer. It had only one hop left, and it touched Jandik's armor. By then all it did was crackle. The tracker's body didn't move, and the chain stopped there.

It was all Vargussel could do not to jump for joy.

Oh, he thought, to the Abyss with it.

He jumped for joy.

The spell he stored in the shield guardian had worked better than he had any reason to hope it would. Chain lightning was a powerful spell but it could be finicky and unpredictable. Though it had spent much of its energy on meat hooks and, at least by the sound of it, shattering the stairs behind Regdar, it had killed all of the watchmen, wounded Regdar himself, and knocked the young mage momentarily senseless.

Vargussel laughed out loud. Killing them was enough but to do it so spectacularly pleased him to no end.

Regdar? the woman called weakly.

Vargussel watched her crawl to the top of the stairs. She peered into the mist but her eyes settled on nothing.

Naull, the lord constable replied. Vargussel liked the sound of his voice. It was weak, quavering. *Is anyone else alive?*

No, the woman answered.

Vargussel laughed again and squeezed the amulet.

Kill them, he commanded the shield guardian. *Kill them slowly. . . .*

Regdar's heart sank at the news that he had lost his entire patrol but he didn't have time to grieve.

The huge shadow in the mist stepped forward, turning at the waist and shoulders, and it pulled back one massive arm. Regdar, knowing it was about to strike him, stepped in the direction of the blow, his own arms back, holding his greatsword over his right shoulder and waiting for the thing's arm to come to him.

The behemoth obliged, and the punch came fast and straight at Regdar. The lord constable set his jaw, narrowed his eyes, waited half a heartbeat, then slashed at the thing's wrist.

When his heavy, enchanted steel blade met the creature's wrist, the impact sent waves of painful vibrations through Regdar's arms, then the rest of his body. His eyes snapped shut and tears squeezed through the lids. He became conscious of each of his ten fingers peeling off the pommel of the greatsword one at a time. The punch never landed, though, and he knew that even though the impact had twisted the sword out of his grip, he'd felt resistance before it came to a full stop. He'd cut the thing.

Regdar let himself fall and rolled away as soon as his back hit the floor. There was a deafening thud when the thing's foot came down, and the floor shook under him, but Regdar kept rolling.

He opened his eyes just as he rolled out of the mist. He blinked at the corpse of Lem, the watchman's eyes ruined, his armor scorched, but Regdar had the wherewithal to take up the enchanted long sword that had once belonged to Lorec and done Lem no good at all. Regdar smelled smoke. He craned his neck to see a black, sooty cloud billowing up from the ruined platform.

Fire, he thought, like we don't have enough to worry about.

"Regdar!" Naull screamed from above.

The lord constable looked up and saw Naull peering over the splintered edge of the platform at him, a nasty burn reddening one side of her face.

"Can you walk?" he shouted to her.

Naull nodded.

"Can you cast?" he asked next.

She nodded again. Regdar was about to tell her to wait for the thing to come out of the mist when a huge hand of steel reached out of the wall of fog and wrapped itself around Regdar's head.

He heard Naull scream his name again, but that was quickly drowned out by the rush of blood in his head. Regdar heard something squeak and was terrified to realize that it was his own jaw. He pulled in a breath and managed to actually get some air, but the inhalation was quickly forced out of him when the behemoth jerked him toward itself.

Regdar didn't want to imagine what the thing meant to do—squeeze his head off if he was lucky, eat him slowly if he wasn't. Not willing to wait and find out, Regdar whirled the long sword in his right hand and dragged it across the beast's wrist. When the blade slipped into a gap, which Regdar trusted was the wound from his own greatsword, he yanked the blade up and into the wound.

Lorec's enchanted blade was sharp indeed, so that even as the thing increased the crushing pressure on Regdar's head, the warrior managed to saw through its wrist until its hand popped off.

Regdar fell. The weight of the thing's hand nearly broke his neck. He had no choice but to drop the long sword so he could use both hands to pull the severed hand from his head.

After watching Regdar being dragged back into the fog by his head, Naull scrambled to her feet and ran to the stairs. She almost fell on her face trying to stop when she remembered the lightning bolt and the sound of exploding wood. She couldn't see through the fog but she had every reason to believe that the stairs weren't there anymore.

Groaning from a pain in her hip that stabbed at her when she stepped back the way she came, Naull ran three long strides, then dived for the rope that Lem and Samoth had used to climb down from the platform. She tightened her grip on the rope and would have closed her eyes if she could. Instead she had to settle for telling herself over and over again: It's not so high. It's not so high. It's not so high.

She forced fear-stiffened legs over the edge of the collapsed platform. When her full weight fell off the edge, she started sliding down the rope. The rough hemp burned what felt like an inch-deep gouge in her palms, and Naull's first impulse was to let go. She fought that and managed to squeeze the rope tighter, hoping to stop the painful slide. Instead, she just slid a bit more slowly, and her hands started to shake. Though Naull meant to squeeze even tighter, her hands opened on their own and she fell.

Eyes closed, jaw clamped shut, Naull braced for an impact that didn't come as quickly as she'd hoped. In truth she was in the air for less than a full second, but Naull felt as if she had an eternity to imagine what it would feel like hitting the floor—and she hit.

There was a cracking sound she hoped wasn't her leg breaking, a sudden stop, the feeling that her feet were caught in something, then a twisting cramp in her neck when she had to stop her head from snapping back onto the flagstone floor.

Groaning through clenched jaws against the pain in her neck, her side, and her hands, Naull tried to stand. She kicked at whatever was holding her feet and felt the sole of her left boot catch on something. When she pushed as hard as she could with her left leg, something snapped—wood—and pain cascaded up her right leg.

Spinning on her rear, she slid off the pile of broken, slowly burning wood and came to rest looking down at her leg. A huge splinter as big around as two of Naull's fingers protruded from her right leg, just above the ankle. Blood seeped out around it.

Another loud boom echoed from the fog, and Naull heard steel scrape against steel. That was all she needed to hear to remind her of the stakes, and she did her best to push the pain from her mind. She stood and found that her leg would still hold weight but the feeling of the jagged wood in her skin sent cold tendrils up her spine.

There was more smoke than fire from the rotten, damp wood smoldering around her, and Naull coughed. She held a hand over her nose and mouth, squinted in the stinging smoke, and was just able to breathe.

Naull limped past the body of Lem, not looking at the watchman. She started casting a spell even before she crossed the abrupt threshold of the roiling mist. Only two steps in, she saw two humanoid shapes. One was easily eight feet tall, so she aimed her spell at that one.

Three bolts of blue-green light shot from her outstretched hand and whizzed unerringly at the giant shadow. When they hit the creature, they burst in flashes of blue light, and the thing rocked back. It put one foot behind it, steadying itself with a great thud.

I hurt it, she thought, but not badly enough.

The smaller shadow—Regdar, but with a too-small sword—took advantage of Naull's attack to slash three times at the thing's legs. One blow connected with a steel-on-steel sound that set Naull's teeth on edge. Sparks arced through the fog

The behemoth answered the slash with a kick that knocked Regdar back on his heels. Naull gasped, sure that her lover was about to fall backward and equally sure that he was dead.

A low growl rattled deep in Vargussel's throat as he peered through the spell, focusing and unfocusing his eyes on the conjured image in a vain attempt to see through his own obscuring fog.

"Damn it all," he grumbled aloud.

He tried every trick of the spell he could to make out more detail, to shift his perspective closer, higher, lower, around to the left, back to the right, waiting for any detail to reveal itself. He could see that one of the shield guardian's hands was missing, and that worried Vargussel as much as it infuriated him.

The spell that the young mage cast when she stepped into the fog was a simple one that revealed her relative level of expertise, but it had managed to further damage his construct.

Time to end it, Vargussel thought.

Closing his eyes, wrapping his fingers tightly around the amulet, the mage sent a new set of instructions to the shield guardian, along with a mental image of Regdar.

The rod, he sent. *The death ray. Now!*

Regdar rolled away the second he hit the floor and managed to just barely avoid the thing's massive foot, which slammed onto the flagstones less than an inch from his left hip. Without bothering to stand, Regdar slashed at the creature's leg and left a good-sized gash in its calf. His sword stopped when it met the solid steel shinbone within. Fearing the worst, Regdar tried yanking the sword from the behemoth's leg only once. The blade didn't budge so Regdar let go. A gouge across the thing's steel thigh struck Regdar's eye. It was the scar he'd given it at the Thrush and the Jay.

I'll kill it piece by piece, he told himself, if I have to.

He scanned the floor for his greatsword while keeping one eye on the behemoth. The monster stepped back and brought its only remaining hand up to its shoulder. It looked to Regdar as if the beast meant to draw a greatsword of its own, and the prospect of facing the thing armed made Regdar redouble his efforts at finding the sword.

Regdar knew that the magic that had briefly staggered the thing must have come from Naull. He could see her shadowy outline deep in the fog. She was well enough away from the thing that—

—there it was!

Leaving any thought of decorum far behind, Regdar scurried, crawled, rolled, and squirmed his way to his fallen blade. His fingers wrapped around the pommel, and he looked up at his opponent. It was indeed drawing a weapon of some sort from its back but in the dense fog it was impossible for Regdar to see in detail exactly what it was. It looked like a staff made of steel—no, not steel, platinum. The behemoth leveled the rod at Regdar as if it was taking aim with a crossbow.

Regdar scrambled to his feet and kept his heavy blade in front of him, momentarily unsure what to do. He heard Naull begin the nonsensical chant of a spell.

The two things that happened next were indistinguishable in Regdar's mind, so perfectly were they timed.

A blinding flash of light illuminated the fog around them so that Regdar felt as if he was bathing in its luminescence—and Naull was in front of him. She hadn't stepped in front of him or jumped in front of him. She was just there, between Regdar and the burst of light. Naull's body flashed in perfect silhouette before him. He heard a sort of thump, like something heavy but soft hitting the floor after a long fall, but it wasn't Naull falling.

The young mage froze as if a great, invisible hand reached up from the ground, stopped her in mid step, and crushed her in its grip. Regdar heard her bones snapping, her breath being forced from her lungs. Her flesh quivered and stretched over ribs that snapped under the force of her own constricting muscles like dry twigs in a giant's hand.

Regdar wanted to scream, or cry, or do anything, but he couldn't. All he could do was wait the few short seconds it took his reeling mind to realize that the woman he loved was dead.

Again.

Vargussel's body was locked in a spasm of conflicting emotions as he watched the lord constable go berserk.

Blood pounded in the wizard's head, and the scrying spell darkened, faded with every fevered heartbeat. Regdar's huge sword became a blur in the fog, moving so fast and so hard that whirls of vapor spun around its tip. The shield guardian hit at the blade, blocked the slashes, hacks, and jabs as best it could, but managed to turn away less than a third of the lord constable's furious attacks.

The scrying spell darkened again but didn't brighten.

Regdar thrust his greatsword through the shield guardian's chest, burying the blade in steel up to the hand guard. The construct's arms quivered at its side. Its chin turned up, and its head slowly lolled to one side.

The scrying spell lasted just long enough for Regdar's bellowing battle cry to echo in Vargussel's head, just long enough for the wizard to see his shield guardian fall, the death ray still clutched in its dead hand.

The spell was gone, and Vargussel's sight blurred, spun, then came to rest in the very real surrounds of his private study.

The wizard clenched his teeth and slammed a fist onto his desk. The lord constable had not only survived but had destroyed the shield guardian. The death ray was in an enemy's hands, and all of it would lead back to Vargussel soon enough. He had very few options left, but all of them spilled into his head at once.

Already muttering the words to a spell that would grant him the gift of flight, Vargussel grabbed his staff and pouches and ran from his study to the nearest exit, a high balcony he rarely visited, where he took to the sky.

Ahead of Vargussel was the stinking sprawl of the Trade Quarter and the only man in New Koratia who could destroy him.

Regdar dragged Naull's body out of the fog and smoke and sat with her. With tears streaming down his face, his body racked with pain and sick, desperate grief, all he could do was sit for as long as it took him to start breathing again. He didn't bother speaking. She couldn't hear him, even if he could put what he felt into words.

She couldn't hear him but there were people who could.

Regdar reminded himself of his position, of where he was, and of the resources at his command. Naull died in the service of the duke. She was the future wife of the lord constable. That had to confer some privileges.

Regdar dragged himself to his feet, sheathed his greatsword, and hefted the limp body. He hated the idea of slinging her over his shoulder like a sack but it was the easiest, fastest way to get her away from the slaughterhouse—and he had to get her out of there. The lord constable had no idea how Naull had so suddenly come between him and the behemoth. He had to assume that she used her magic to appear between them in some silly effort to shield him. He had never seen her do that before but her spells always struck Regdar as a confusing bag of tricks, sometimes unreliable, frequently running dry at the worst times. Ultimately, one of those spells allowed her to make a rash decision that cost her her life.

Regdar scanned the huge room and saw that the fog was fading away. An old, stone ramp rose from the center of the room, ending in a fall of timbers, brick, and plaster at the ceiling. The bottom of the ramp emptied into the wooden chutes. The place was a slaughterhouse, and the cattle must have been driven down the ramp from the street above, through the chutes, to be killed at the end of each passage. Their carcasses then were hefted up on meat hooks and rolled along tracks to the butchers. Underground, the disturbing sounds and smells of the killing floor would be hidden from the city around it, and the whole affair would take up less valuable space.

He turned toward the ramp, seeking the most direct path back to the street, but stopped long enough to spare a glance at the thing that had murdered so many of the city's best people.

It was a made thing, not a living being, put together mostly with steel. It was dead, whatever that meant in its case, but there was no blood. Its only adornment was a steel carving on its chest, inlaid with two rubies. The rubies formed the eyes of what might have been a dog, a bear, a horse, or some other animal's face. Regdar's eyes stopped on the carving. He'd seen it before. That stylized, simple, but distinctive shape with its two rubies was familiar, but from where?

Regdar stepped closer to the dead construct and his eyes settled on the platinum rod still gripped in its remaining hand. That bar was pointed at him when the flash went off—the flash that killed Naull.

"It's not the behemoth," Regdar muttered, thinking aloud.

Groaning with pain, and careful not to drop Naull's body, Regdar squatted and slid the platinum rod out of the dead thing's hand. It wasn't easy but he managed to secure the rod in the straps of his pack, against his scabbard.

The behemoth wasn't the murder weapon, he concluded silently. The behemoth wielded the murder weapon.

Regdar turned to the ramp again with Naull hanging from his shoulders, and he started climbing. Already her body was growing cold.

The jumble of structures so far below him confused Vargussel, and it took him a precious few minutes more than he expected to find the slaughterhouse. When it came clear below him, Vargussel dropped from the sky onto the street in front of the dilapidated structure. From above, Vargussel could see that the slaughterhouse was crawling with watchmen. Most were just milling around, waving on the occasional passerby who paused to wonder what they were doing.

A few of the watchmen took note of the wizard slowly descending from the deep gray sky, drenched in the rain that fell around him. They drew their swords but stepped back, afraid and on guard. One of them, a sergeant, stepped forward and as Vargussel's feet came to rest on the cobblestones, the watchman approached him. The wizard didn't recognize the sergeant but the man seemed to know him. The sergeant sheathed his sword and gave a shallow, fast bow.

"Are you in command here?" Vargussel asked.

"No," the sergeant replied. "I mean, no, sir, not really. My men are charged with containing this corner of the building."

"Do you know who I am?" the wizard asked.

"Lord Vargussel?" the sergeant replied.

"Correct," said the wizard, "and I have been sent by the duke with new orders."

"Sir?" the sergeant asked. "That's not usually the way we—"

"Did you see me fly here, Sergeant?" Vargussel interrupted, letting his impatience show in all its force. "Of course this isn't usual but I was sent as quickly as my spells would carry me because the news is grim indeed."

"Sir?"

"The murderer has been found out," Vargussel said, "and he is in the basement of that building, even now carrying out his most heinous crime to date."

The sergeant smiled dully, and said, "That's fine, sir. Lord Constable Regdar himself is down there already. You don't have to worry about—"

"I will decide what I worry about, Sergeant," Vargussel snapped, "and the duke will decide what he worries about. What worries us both now is the lord constable himself."

"Sir?"

"He is the murderer, son," Vargussel said. "It's Regdar!"

The sergeant's mouth opened, which only made him look more stupid.

"Tell the others!" Vargussel shouted, and the sergeant jumped.

As the watchman relayed the scandalous lie about their lord constable, Vargussel stepped closer to the building. He'd heard something just as the sergeant ran off—wood scraping on stone? When he leaned closer to the stinking ruin, he heard it again.

It sounded like someone was digging around in there.

When dust blew into Regdar's lungs, he coughed. When rusty nails scored his flesh, he winced. When splinters nicked his eyes, he blinked. When his muscles protested under a particularly heavy fall of wreckage, he grunted. When Naull's body slipped in his grasp, he held her tighter.

That's how he dug himself out of the ruin below and into the ruin above.

Some of his men, whom he only vaguely remembered stationing there, stood around him in a ring. By the looks on their faces, he thought he must actually look like the grave robber he felt like.

"Help me," Regdar grunted.

One watchman stepped forward, his sword drawn.

"Take her," Regdar said.

The man didn't move.

"What's wrong with you?" asked Regdar as his feet finally came clear of the rubble.

"Lord Constable . . ." the watchman said, but seemed unable to finish.

The watchmen all looked at each other as if waiting for someone to make the first move.

Footsteps ground toward him through the ruin. Regdar looked up to see the duke's wizard stomping at him with purpose.

"Vargussel . . ." Regdar started, trailing off when his eyes fell on the amulet.

Swinging from a chain around Vargussel's neck was the same stylized dog with ruby eyes. The sign of the behemoth. The sign of the death ray. The sign of the murderer.

Regdar's head spun, and his vision went red with rage.

For the time it took Regdar to gently lay Naull's body on the broken timbers, he let his emotions run wild. Vargussel continued to approach. The watchmen formed a ring around them both but seemed paralyzed with indecision.

By the time Regdar stood, he'd settled his mind around the imminent fight to the death with the powerful wizard. His mind slipped into trained patterns of matching information to tactics. The wizard stopped several paces away and was waving the watchmen closer, commanding their attention.

The behemoth had injured Regdar, and his climb through the wreckage of the slaughterhouse only weakened him further. While one part of Regdar wanted to draw his greatsword and hew through the wizard like a farmer reaping wheat, the soldier in him knew he had a few moments to help himself enter the coming contest, if not at an advantage, then with less of a disadvantage. He reached into a pouch at his belt and drew out a cool, steel vial.

"Hear me, men of the watch!" Vargussel called, his voice echoing in the narrow streets of the Trade Quarter. "I have come on the orders of the duke himself."

Regdar ignored the lie. Instead, with his hand behind his leg where it was hidden from the wizard's sight, he picked the wax seal off the vial.

"The murderer has revealed himself!" Vargussel shouted.

Regdar popped the cork from the vial. Vargussel pointed an accusing finger at him.

"It is Regdar!" the wizard screeched.

Regdar downed the potion in a single gulp. A nervous murmur rose from the watchmen and the gathering crowd of onlookers alike.

Regdar tossed the empty steel vial to the ground. Waves of warmth flowed through him. His pain turned to an itch, then went away. Not all of his considerable injuries were healed by the potion but Regdar felt strong again, and he had two more such vials anyway. He hadn't expected a fight at the top of the ramp or he would have downed at least one before climbing out. He expected to fall into the arms of his own men and rely on his position as lord constable to have his wounds tended to later.

As Regdar drew his greatsword, Vargussel chanted through a spell, waving his hands over his own body. The wizard burst into flames, and the surrounding watchmen all stepped back, some gasping with surprise or fear. The flames settled into a smoldering blue and orange incandescence that played over the wizard's robes, his face, and his hands. Vargussel's teeth were clenched tightly shut, his eyes narrowed to slits, his face reddened with fury. Regdar was sure his own face mirrored the wizard's.

The lord constable stepped within a blade's length of the wizard and slashed across the burning man's midsection. The tip of Regdar's blade should have cut Vargussel deeply enough to spill his entrails but it bounced and skittered across flames that had a strange solidity. A flash of white-hot light forced Regdar to close his eyes and step back. Pain blazed across his face. He knew he was burned but didn't care. He heard Vargussel scuffle backward as well.

Though his face hurt, Regdar opened his eyes and was happy to see that his vision was unimpaired. He wasn't happy to see the wizard's staff descending on him too fast for Regdar to block.

The staff didn't strike him hard. It would have bounced off his armor with hardly a grunt from Regdar were the staff not enchanted. Tendrils of blue-green lightning played along Regdar's armor and made his shoulder and neck convulse painfully. It was startlingly close to the pain he'd felt from the behemoth's lightning, but less intense.

The wizard swung the staff quickly for a second strike but Regdar was ready. He batted the weapon away with the flat of his sword. A shower of sparks cascaded around the blade and Regdar felt his fingers tingle on the pommel.

"You die now, Lord Constable," Vargussel sneered.

Regdar didn't bother replying. Instead, he swept his greatsword in a wide arc, intending to decapitate the wizard and end the fight quickly. Something about the way Vargussel moved toward the blow made Regdar change his mind. At the last possible moment, Regdar twisted the sword in his grip so that it missed the still-smoldering wizard by less than an inch. The spell would have burned him again.

Regdar stepped back to give himself time to think, and Vargussel did the same. Instead of thinking, though, the wizard cast another spell. Hoping to interrupt it, Regdar stomped in with an overhand hack that crashed down onto the crown of Vargussel's head.

The blade met resistance for only a split second before the wizard was gone. Regdar heard him laugh with a harsh, scornful sound, and he stepped back again. There were eight Vargussels arrayed before the fighter. The one whose skull Regdar just split open would have been the ninth. The group of Vargussels kept in motion, wandering around each other, identical in every way down to the finest detail.

"One of them is you," the fighter grumbled.

All eight of the wizards laughed, and all eight replied, "But which one?"

"Let's find out," Regdar said.

The lord constable charged again. The false wizards scattered, stepping in circles to confuse him even as they all cast a spell in perfect harmony. All eight of them pointed to Regdar, and all eight shared the gleam of triumph in their eyes.

The spell sent cramping pain pounding through Regdar's body. His chest burned when his heart seemed to skip a beat. His vision blurred, then went black, and he stumbled, trying to get suddenly ungainly feet under him. He managed not to fall but could do little else as he rode out the blasts of agonizing torment.

At the moment he was sure was his last, when he believed he couldn't take another second of the magical abuse, the pain was gone. Regdar drew in a deep breath and forced his eyes to focus on any one of the eight wizards.

Vargussel and his images had backed off, giving Regdar room to drop dead or giving the wizard room for a spell that would finish him off.

Regdar could hardly breathe. Facing a host of bad alternatives, he decided to drink another potion. Vargussel wasn't interested in taking Regdar alive, because they obviously both knew who was the real murderer. Why else would Vargussel be there trying to kill him? The wizard couldn't let the lord constable live any more than Regdar could suffer Vargussel breathing air meant for Naull. It was a fight to the death.

The wizard cast his spell, mimicked perfectly by his seven duplicates, as Regdar ripped the cork off the second vial. He drew it to his lips. The eight Vargussels thrust their hands toward Regdar, and it was as if a giant hand picked up the lord constable and threw him. Regdar saw no hand, felt barely a whisper of pressure against his body, but fly through the air he did.

The steel vial stayed in his grip but the contents shot out of the container in a stream. Regdar, rather than try to control the way he landed, used every bit of agility he could muster to get his open mouth in front of that healing stream.

The sweet elixir splashed against his lips. He whirled his tongue to get every drop. He swallowed even as his back slammed into the ground. Regdar held his breath, held down the potion, and lay there squirming as new pain met the potion's healing effects and his body quivered.

Regdar climbed to his feet, dragging his sword off the ground. The healing effect of the potion made him stronger with every beat of his heart. By the time he stood straight, sword at the ready, he was strong and determined again.

"That's two healing potions you owe me," Regdar said.

Vargussel paled momentarily. The flames that licked across his skin were fading away. Regdar couldn't understand the first few words of the wizard's reply, then he realized that Vargussel was casting another spell. Before Regdar could charge, a globe of shimmering light encircled all eight Vargussels, and all eight smiled at him—laughed at him—and started casting again.

The lord constable charged the wizard but again failed to reach him before the spell took effect. Regdar chose the nearest incarnation of Vargussel and slashed at him but the wizard wasn't where he was supposed to be. At first Regdar assumed he'd dispelled another conjured image but the wizard's laugh was coming from—

Regdar looked up and saw all eight Vargussels floating in the air above him. The wizard hadn't disappeared, he'd jumped into the air and stayed there. Regdar guessed the wizard was two dozen feet above the ruined building, well out of reach.

"You were inconvenient, Lord Constable," all eight Vargussels called down to him, "then you became troublesome, then you became costly. Now you're just meat."

Regdar smiled and sheathed his greatsword in the scabbard on his back. He reached behind him and slipped a hand under his pack.

"Watchmen!" the wizard screamed. "Kill this man, in the name of the Duke of Koratia!"

None of the watchmen moved. Regdar drew out a leather satchel that had been strapped under his pack.

"Is that it?" Vargussel called down. "Is that the weapon you used to kill the heirs of New Koratia?"

The lord constable opened the satchel and pulled from it what looked like a bundle of sticks—albeit sticks of beautifully carved, stained, and polished wood.

"What have you got there?" the wizard asked, his eyes narrowing, his head tipped to one side. "What is that?"

With a flick of his wrist the bundle of sticks snapped out and together to form a sturdy composite bow.

Vargussel flinched, then smiled, his eight faces occasionally distorting behind the globe of shimmering light.

Regdar strung the bow, all the while waiting for Vargussel to hurl another spell at him. No spell came. The watchmen stood their ground. It was as if everyone wanted to see Regdar shoot all eight wizards out of the sky, one by one.

"Weapons," the wizard mused from eight mouths. "Always weapons."

Regdar slipped a beautifully fletched arrow from his quiver, nocked it, drew back the bowstring, aimed, and fired while Vargussel rasped out another spell.

Regdar's arrow passed Vargussel's lightning bolt like carts on a crowded city thoroughfare. The arrow struck true, and another of the false Vargussels popped away into thin air, leaving only seven.

The lightning bolt struck true as well but there was only one Regdar. The pain was worse than the construct's lightning, far worse than the wizard's staff. Regdar's body went rigid, and he felt himself lifted off his feet. His hair didn't just stand on end, it twisted and pulled. His armor felt like pans left in a fiery oven, the different pieces clanking against each other as he quaked.

It lasted less than a second then was gone, leaving only the stench of scalded flesh, burnt hair, and ozone. Regdar's armor creaked and groaned as it cooled and popped back into place.

Regdar drew a second arrow.

"Go ahead," the wizard chided, "stand there."

Regdar nocked the arrow, pulled back the bowstring, and aimed. The images had pulled a wand from under their robes, and seven sticks of crimson gold were leveled at Regdar. He fired, and so did Vargussel.

It was a line of roiling orange flame, drawn together by some arcane force, that flowed at Regdar from seven identical wands. Having loosed his arrow, Regdar was able to turn, hunch his shoulders, and let the fire pour over his armored back. The heat burned him, the fire blistered his skin, the pain weakened him—but he didn't fall.

He turned, and only six Vargussels remained.

All were pointing the wand at him again.

Regdar consciously decided to jump when he was already in midair, halfway between where he'd been standing and anywhere else within jumping distance.

Fire poured down onto that spot from the floating wizard, setting the rotting timbers on fire. The damp wood smoldered, giving off an odorous, greasy smoke. Regdar looked quickly around and saw the leaning remnant of a wall. It wasn't much but any cover was better than nothing, when he was already burned, cut, shocked, bruised, and bleeding. He needed a moment to think.

Regdar stood and ran, sometimes skipping, sometimes leaping over jumbled piles of debris. He had to make a nerve-racking detour but he passed close enough to Naull's body to scoop the corpse up in one hand and continue.

Another wave of magical fire rumbled behind him, sending up more black smoke that Regdar hoped might conceal him from the wizard's wrath. He felt the heat on his back but managed to outrun the flame. At last he hopped behind the wall and cringed, expecting another blast of fire, but it didn't come.

"Run, Regdar!" Vargussel shrieked, his voice echoing over the ruin with the six-part harmony of the conjured images. "Prove your guilt for all to see! Take that last victim and run!"

Ignoring the ranting wizard, Regdar pulled the last of the steel vials from his pack, peeled off the sealing wax, popped the cork, and downed the sweet contents before he could talk himself out of it. The burns were too painful, and he could feel that the lightning had damaged something inside his gut. He had no choice. He would just have to be smarter.

"What's the matter, Vargussel?" Regdar called back to the wizard. "Did I upset you?"

"Silence, murdering dog!" the wizard shot back.

Regdar drew an arrow and nocked it, then moved a few steps along the wall.

"That monster must have cost a pretty penny," the lord constable taunted. "Sorry I had to kill it."

Regdar found a hole big enough to see through, and he scanned the sky for the Vargussels.

"Bastard!" the wizard shouted, a thin, reedy edge to his voice. "You have no idea what it took to create that masterpiece. You have no idea what it means to build something. You, who kill and kill and kill until that boot-shining moron of a duke hands you the duchy on a silver platter—hands you Maelani like he's selling you a goat."

Maelani? Regdar thought. What could she have to do with all this?

Fire washed over the broken wall. Regdar barely ducked in time before flames licked through the hole he was looking through. He avoided getting burned, but when he looked out again, all he could see was thick, black smoke.

"You have something of mine, lord constable," Vargussel called, letting the title drip with contempt. "The rod. Give it to me and I'll kill you quickly."

The rod?

Regdar shook his head. Rage and pain had slowed the parts of his brain that he found himself in need of but his intellect came back to him fast enough. The rod the wizard was talking about must be the weapon the behemoth used to kill Naull.

"I have it!" Regdar shouted.

"Give it to me!" demanded the wizard.

Regdar stood and looked through the hole again. He saw two of the six wizards hovering a few yards away, below the crest of the wall. Regdar saw him put the wand away.

"I'll destroy it!" Regdar threatened.

The wizard laughed in response. The thin, reedy edge of his voice made the sound even more unsettling.

"You couldn't begin to know how to destroy that rod, you drooling deficient," the wizard replied. "It's not a stick to be snapped over your knee. It's an item of power your mind couldn't even—"

"I'll use it, then," Regdar interrupted.

There was a long pause, then the wizard's voice rang over the ruins again, low and threatening. "In all your pitiful, mundane, blade-polishing existence, you couldn't muster the psychic resources necessary to call forth that weapon's power. Your tiny brain couldn't hold that much hate."

Hate? Regdar thought.

"I'll take it out of your scorched, ruined, dead hand," Vargussel said, then he began casting another spell.

A bolt of lightning blasted into the already leaning wall. Regdar dived over Naull's body and put his arms over his head. His hair stood on end again, and his skin crawled uncomfortably but the bolt missed him. The shadow of the wall was gone, however, so he knew he was exposed. He felt the rod, hard and cold against his back. Regdar grabbed it and rolled into the nearest shadow. He clutched the rod in one hand, his bow in the other. Both clattered against the fallen timbers.

The warrior rolled to his feet and stood, back against what remained of the wall. Greasy, black smoke whirled up into the gray sky.

All this, Regdar thought, for a girl?

27

"**You know I'll do what's best** for the duchy," Maelani told her father, "and if that means I must marry sooner rather than later, I'm willing to accept that."

"Are you indeed," the duke replied, settling into a comfortable leather armchair.

Swirling the fine elven cognac in an oversize snifter, the duke took in a long breath through his nose, letting the heady aroma of the spirit waft through his head. A fire crackled next to him, more a bonfire than a simple hearth fire in the massive, marble fireplace. He reminded himself regularly that many of New Koratia's citizens made their homes in spaces smaller than that fireplace, and that thought often guided his hand in matters of domestic policy. In matters of the heart, he was at a loss—most of the time.

Maelani sank onto the bearskin rug at his feet, curling up like a young lioness surveying the veldt she'd claimed as her own.

"You'll make a fine duchess," he found himself saying.

Maelani smiled and said, "Like Mother?"

The duke took a small sip of the cognac, letting it burn his bottom lip for a second before swallowing.

"Father?" Maelani prompted, concern creeping into her voice.

"No," he said with a sigh. "No, your mother, may Pelor forever hold her in his embrace, was never much good at it. She was a lord's daughter, to be sure, but her family's estate was a rural one. They were farmers at heart, and it was a farmer's blood that warmed her veins the whole of her days."

"Doesn't that same blood flow in my veins, too?" she asked. "I always loved visiting Grandfather's estate ... the horses, the flowers ..."

The duke laughed cheerfully and said, "You may have enjoyed it for the occasional fortnight's repose, my dear, but even when you were still in diapers, you couldn't wait to get back to the city. You were born a noblewoman and have only grown further into that role since."

"Is that so bad?" she asked with a delicate frown.

The duke shook his head.

Maelani laughed and said, "But my nobility, mixed with a warrior's strength of arm and character...."

The duke took another sip of cognac, a longer one this time, and studied his daughter's face.

"It sounds to me," he said, "as if you've made up your mind about something."

Maelani smiled—a sincere and bright expression—and was about to answer when the door burst open and the elite guard Officer of the Day entered almost at a run.

The duke stood to receive his officer, who slid to a stop and stood at attention.

"Your Highness," the officer said, "there is a disturbance in the city."

The duke glanced back to see Maelani slowly stand, smoothing her gown as she did. He held the snifter out to her and she took it from him.

"Where?" the duke asked.

"The Trade Quarter, sir," the officer reported, "in the ruins of an old slaughterhouse. Your Highness, it seems the murderer has been run to ground."

The duke blinked but began walking to the door with purpose. The elite guard officer fell in behind him, and Maelani followed as well.

"Has the lord constable been advised?" the duke asked as they walked.

"Your Highness . . ." the officer replied, hesitating.

They stepped through into a corridor bustling with elite guard officers and men, their faces betraying anxiety and excitement.

"Where is Lord Constable Regdar?" the duke roared.

"Your Highness," the officer answered, "it has been suggested that the lord constable is the murderer."

The duke stopped dead in his tracks, and the officer almost collided with him. Maelani did in fact lightly bump into the officer, who turned to apologize, his face red. He stopped when the duke's meaty hand fell on his shoulder and turned him back around.

"Who made such an allegation?" the duke asked.

The officer swallowed and said, "Vargussel, Your Highness. They fight to the death even now."

The color drained from the duke's face, and he found it difficult to draw in a breath. His eyes met his daughter's, and she looked the same.

"To the Trade Quarter then," the duke said, "and let's see for ourselves."

Regdar rolled the rod over in his hands. It was surprisingly heavy, heavier even than his greatsword. To Regdar's untrained eye it appeared to be made of solid platinum. The metal alone was worth a king's ransom. The power to kill in a way that left no trace and cut whatever spiritual connection a soul had with its body must have cost even—

Regdar's heart sank. His blood ran cold. He began to sweat and shiver at the same time.

The victims couldn't be brought back.

Families of the murdered young men had tried. They employed the most powerful priests in the city, who had tried every prayer to no avail. Whoever was killed by that beautiful, platinum abomination stayed dead.

Naull would stay dead.

All because a grizzled, old mage lusted after the hand of a girl less than half his age. Or was it the duchy that would be her dowry that Vargussel sought? Did it matter? Not to Regdar.

"Hate . . ." he whispered.

He slipped the rod over his shoulder and wove it between the straps of his pack and scabbard again.

Hate, he thought.

Bending down, he retrieved his bow from the tumble of smoking, rotten timbers.

Hate enough, Regdar thought.

He drew an arrow, nocked it, and pulled back the string as he turned. He looked quickly through one hole in the blasted wall, then another, until he saw the wizard. He needed only a moment to aim through the de facto arrow loop before letting fly.

As the arrow whizzed through the air, Regdar thought he heard it whisper, "Hate," in its wake. In truth the arrow did not speak but the wizard did, mumbling and hissing his way through another incantation.

The arrow popped the wizard's image like a bubble, and it was gone. The others continued their chant.

"Four decoys left," Regdar whispered, "then I'll show you just how much I can hate."

As he spoke, he nocked another arrow, drew, aimed, and—

—was surrounded by a stone wall. The construction appeared out of thin air, circling him in a tight cylinder of rough, gray stone. Regdar drew in a sharp breath, waiting for something worse but in the space of a heartbeat, the wall didn't come down on him, the space didn't fill with fire, acid, or lightning. With the position of the floating wizard fixed in his mind, he lifted his bow up and loosed the arrow.

Regdar dropped the bow and jumped, his arms stretched out over his head. He barely reached the lip but found himself hanging by his fingertips from the top of the stone cylinder. As he lifted himself up, he scanned the sky. When he saw only four identical Vargussels floating, casting another spell, Regdar knew his last arrow had sailed true. Only three more images to go before the real Vargussel would be revealed.

Regdar pulled himself up high enough that one knee touched the top of the wall as the wizard's chant came to an end.

The wall began to collapse. No, not collapse but melt, droop, like a stick of butter thrust into an oven.

The knee that Regdar had hoisted atop the wall sank into cool mud. He tried to jump over the edge but, when he pushed off with his hands, he succeeded only in burying them up to his elbows in mud. He slipped back and managed to get his left hand free. Looking down, he saw that the whole cylinder was sinking into a formless mound of gray-brown mud. His feet twisted around each other, his right arm pulled painfully past his side and behind his back. The mud pressed relentlessly against him, drawing him down.

Regdar grabbed the end of the platinum rod with his left hand and slipped it free of the straps. It wasn't easy with the mud drawing it down but fortunately the liquefying stone didn't cling to the metal. He drew the rod like a sword and held it over his head in an attempt to keep it, and his arm, out of the mud for as long as possible.

Finally, the slow, crushing descent came to an end. Regdar found himself buried up to the neck in thick, claylike mud. He couldn't move, could barely breathe.

Regdar watched the wizard and his three duplicates slowly descend from the sky. The instant their feet touched the rubble-strewn ground, all four of them strode toward Regdar with a purpose.

All four of them were laughing.

As accustomed as she had become to magical travel, Maelani found her hands shaking and her knees weak as she stepped into the circle with her father and a pair of his elite guard. It was rare that she and her father were together outside the confines of the palace. The duchy could survive the death of either one but losing both would cause a power vacuum and probably a civil war.

Still, she was surprised at how easy it had been to convince her father to take her along with him to see the "fight to the death" between Regdar and Vargussel. He had seen in her eyes, she was sure, her love for the lord constable. She made no effort to mask it. Her choice was made, and she knew her father not only concurred but had bluntly maneuvered Regdar in front of her in the first place.

As Maelani waited for the assembled officers and palace staffers to activate various and sundry magical items that would speed them on their way and likely cloak them in layer upon layer of protective magic as well, she closed her eyes and tried to imagine why Vargussel would make such a scandalous, unbelievable claim. Who of sane mind could believe that Regdar was the murderer?

The truth hit Maelani like a bucket of cold water poured over her head. Her eyes popped open and she turned to her father to tell him.

Before she could speak, the world turned upside down, went black, then gray, then inside out. Lights flashed. She heard a sound like a song, thin and reedy, but devoid of melody, and felt a sprinkle of chill rain.

She realized her eyes were closed. When she opened them again, they had arrived.

The sky was a dark, threatening gray, dripping cold drizzle. Wind whipped down the narrow Trade Quarter street and chilled Maelani to the bone. She wrapped her arms around herself and blinked, getting her bearings after the brief slip from reality.

Her father was already moving, already talking, already issuing orders. City watchmen gave hurried, clipped reports, deferring to the elite guard, bowing, walking backward. She followed, an elite guardsman with a halberd dogging her tracks. She'd walked under guard before and knew that the man with the polearm was well-trained, well-paid, and fiercely loyal. He was there for the express purpose of trading his life to protect hers. The thought made Maelani wonder how many men there were in the city, in all the duchy, who would do that. How many already had?

"Father," she called through the press of watchmen and soldiers. "Father!"

The duke turned to glance at her but kept walking.

"Father," she persisted, "it's Vargussel."

He glanced back at her again and asked, "What are you saying?"

"It's Vargussel," Maelani repeated. "He is the murderer, not Regdar."

The duke didn't miss a step. He kept on, following the watchmen around a half-collapsed wall. It was then that Maelani detected the faint stench of decay, of rotten meat, that was draped over the place like a shawl. She put a hand to her lips but quickly took it away.

"It was because of me," she said.

This got the attention of several of the men-at-arms, if not the duke himself.

"It was because of—" she started to repeat but stopped when they stepped around the wall and saw Regdar buried to his neck in mud and four identical wizards marching toward him with grim determination.

Maelani had to shake her head and blink twice before her mind would accept what she saw. The four wizards all looked exactly like Vargussel. They walked the same way, were dressed the same way, and all four were casting a spell. The words, their meaning unfamiliar to Maelani, came out of all four mouths at the same time, with the same tone and cadence. All four of them moved their hands in precisely the same intricate pattern.

"Stop him!" Maelani shouted, and her father finally turned to her. She spoke to him. "Vargussel killed all those young men because he didn't want them to marry me."

"Why wouldn't he . . . ?" asked the duke, though she could tell he was already working out the reasoning in his mind.

"Vargussel has made it plain that he intended to have my hand," she said, though the thought of it made her ill. "He killed those men, and will kill Regdar now, because they were competing for the same prize."

"Your hand," the duke said, then turned to the wizards and his lord constable. "The duchy."

The four identical Vargussels finished their incantation and converged on Regdar, one hand thrust forward as if to grab the lord constable by the top of his head.

"Vargussel!" the duke roared. His voice rolled across the ruin like thunder but the wizards didn't stop, didn't even glance at the duke. "Stop, Vargussel! In the name of New Koratia!"

But Vargussel didn't stop. All four of them converged on Regdar, and all four of them grabbed the top of his head, fingers sliding under the lord constable's helm.

Regdar, who was buried to the neck in a mound of gray-brown mud, twisted and quivered. Maelani heard a crackling, buzzing sound, and saw sparks dance along the slick surface of the mud pile. Those same sparks danced along the legs of the quartet of wizards, and when they touched each in turn, that wizard disappeared into thin air. First one, then another, then a third, until only one Vargussel remained, twitching and grimacing himself.

The lone wizard stepped back—staggered really—and Regdar's head slumped forward. Only one of the lord constable's arms was free of the mud. Maelani puzzled at the rod of what appeared to be platinum he clutched in his free hand. Regdar's head rolled back so that he was looking up at the sky. His eyes were red, his face pale.

Vargussel shook himself and stared down at Regdar with undisguised hate. Maelani found herself stepping backward, and she only stopped when the elite guard with the halberd put a hand gently on her arm.

The power, she thought. To bury Lord Constable Regdar, to sap his strength with the pain of burning spells, to kill him in front of the duke, the watch, and the elite guard....

Maelani watched her behavior toward the old wizard play back in her mind in a cascade of petty humiliations and catty dismissals. Never had it occurred to her that the man was capable not only of murder but murder on an unprecedented scale directed at the very heart of the duchy. She almost wretched when she realized how badly the hideous monstrosity of a man wanted her, the lengths to which he was willing to go, and the horrifying power at his command.

For the first time in years, Maelani felt every bit the helpless, ignorant little girl.

Regdar could breathe but only with small, childlike, panting gasps. Pain had settled down to a dull, humming numbness. Blood rushed in his ears. The mud pressed on him, squeezed him, and chilled him. Regdar couldn't remember a time when he'd been so cold.

He looked up at the gray sky because he couldn't keep his neck from bending that direction. The chilly drizzle stung his eyes, and he blinked. As if that movement alone was enough to move his head, he found his neck turning, his head rolling down. On the way he saw Vargussel standing over him and took note that there was only one of him. The wizard's shock must have traveled through the wet mud with enough energy to dispel the last of the images.

"You did it . . ." Regdar coughed out, "to yourself . . . that time."

"Give me what is mine," the wizard said.

His voice was strong, steady, and confident. He might have been tickled by that last spell, it might have been enough to dispel his conjured doppelgangers, but otherwise he was fine.

"And I'm dying," Regdar said aloud.

"Yes," the wizard hissed, his voice even more than his words conveying perfect, pure confidence in that truth. "You are dying, Regdar."

The lord constable closed his eyes. In that moment, in the time it took for Vargussel to say those last words, Regdar wondered if it was true. Had he failed?

His patrol had been chopped out from under him to a man. Naull was not just dead but irretrievably so. Had he failed the duke, failed the city, failed the duchy, failed Maelani, failed Naull, and failed himself? The wizard was going to kill him. The next spell, whatever it was, would be enough. The wizard would kill him and be free to make up any story he wanted. He would convince the duke, through guile or spell, that it was Regdar who killed all those people. Vargussel would have Maelani, he would be duke, and ultimately, it would be Regdar who condemned all of Koratia to that fate.

"I don't think so," he said.

Regdar felt his left arm jerk, and instinctively he took a tighter grip on his sword. He opened his eyes and saw that it wasn't his sword he was holding.

Vargussel was trying to pull the rod from his hand.

Regdar coughed, then champed his teeth down. His body shook. He looked up at the wizard's triumphant, gloating, hateful grin, and a fire swept through his body.

Hate.

It was hate that warmed him, hate that made him look Vargussel in the eyes, hate that strengthened his grip, moved his arm, and thrust the platinum rod into the wizard's gut.

Regdar tensed every muscle in his body, drove his very blood forward. He let that hate, that pure contempt, flow from him and into the rod. He let his hate power the death ray.

Vargussel couldn't believe it.

He couldn't believe that Regdar could do it.

He couldn't believe that after all his sacrifices, it came to this.

He couldn't believe he was feeling the same thing the others had.

This is it, he thought. This is what it feels like?

There was a blinding flash of light that illuminated the rain and smoke around them so that Vargussel felt as if he had burst into flame. He heard a dull boom, like something heavy but soft hitting the ground after a long fall. Was that his soul?

Is that my soul falling? he wondered.

The wizard froze, no longer able to feel the rod pressing into his abdomen. It was as if a great, invisible hand had reached up from the ground, grabbed him, and was squeezing him from all directions. His breath was forced from his lungs, and he knew that he'd never draw another one. His flesh quivered and stretched over ribs that snapped under the force of his own constricting muscles. Vargussel felt every bone in his body snapping. He felt every agonizing, burning break, one at a time.

With lungs devoid of air, he couldn't speak, but his mind threw out a desperate call the same way he would send his thoughts, his commands, and his hatred into the shield guardian.

Master . . . help me!

Everything was dark and cold, and Vargussel was alone. He felt nothing but there was a whisper, as faint as the footsteps of a fly:

You have failed me, as you have failed Vecna.

Vargussel wanted to beg, wanted to say anything, argue . . . anything, but he couldn't.

He will be waiting for you, whispered his dark master, *in Hell.*

Epilogue ... Maelani hoped she wouldn't have to attend another state funeral for a long time. Too many had been held of late, and Naull's was the saddest of all. Maelani took her turn at the casket and apologized to the young woman's still, lifeless face, but she knew that would never be enough.

Power had brought on all those funerals; not just the power to kill but the lust for power over others. She had always believed, as the daughter of a duke, that she understood power, but she had come to know that she never really had.

There were two men in her life whose example she thought she followed but had in fact ignored. Her father was comfortable in his power over the duchy because he understood the responsibility he bore to his subjects and to himself. Regdar, who never pursued power and who only reluctantly accepted the title of Lord Constable of New Koratia, had set that aside even before the woman he loved was buried. He had visited the depths of emotion and used the hate that he found there to save them all, but he also surrendered that power at the first opportunity.

Standing at the western gate, surrounded by a ring of elite guardsmen and a crowd of curious commoners behind them, Maelani took what she knew could be her last look at Regdar. The warrior was somber and serious, his face drawn and tight at the same time. His eyes were red but Maelani never saw him shed a tear. As a thousand souls watched in silence, Regdar checked the saddle of the war-horse given him by the duke and took a last stock of his supplies.

The duke approached him, and Regdar turned.

"You didn't fail, Regdar," the duke said, loudly enough so all could hear. "Leaders lose men."

Regdar nodded and said, "I never wanted to be a leader."

"I accept this only as a leave of absence," the duke said. "Return, when you can, and you will be Lord Constable again."

Regdar nodded, and Maelani's breath caught. She could see by his face that that would never be. He had resigned the post, refused the title, and he would never take it up again. He had lost men, like her father had, but Regdar had lost more. He also lost Naull, and Maelani imagined she could see a piece of him missing. When he walked it was as if he was both heavier and yet, somehow, less connected to the ground, less connected to anything—lost.

Regdar looked at her, and Maelani tried to hold his gaze but had to look away. Tears filled her vision but before that, she could see in his face that he didn't blame her. Maelani had a lot to regret and a lot to repair, but Regdar didn't blame her. She also saw that this man who she thought she loved . . . she didn't know what that word meant, and she was beginning to understand that she wouldn't until she found a love like Regdar had. And then, only if she was lucky.

Regdar mounted the horse and took the reins, turning the great beast to face her father again.

"Your Highness," Regdar said, "I take my leave of you, with your permission."

The duke nodded and said, "As reluctant as I am to do so, I grant you your leave."

Regdar nodded but hesitated, looking out through the open gate to the setting sun beyond.

"Where will you go?" the duke asked.

Regdar looked at him and shrugged. With a smile sadder than anything Maelani had ever seen, he said, "West, with the night."

Her father said nothing, and Regdar turned his horse away. When he passed through the gate and was clear of the mighty walls of New Koratia, Regdar spurred the horse to a gallop.

Maelani didn't watch him go. She couldn't. Instead, she drew a vial from her purse, a vial for which she had paid a pretty sum. It was the love potion she so foolishly planned to slip to Regdar. The sight of the witch's brew, much less the thought of it, disgusted her. The sickening potion was what she possessed. Regdar's heart was what Naull had owned.

Maelani opened the vial and poured the contents onto the gravel at her feet.

The duke stepped next to her and asked, "What is that?"

Maelani had to take a second to gather herself before she could answer, "Nothing."

And that was true.

R.A. Salvatore's
War of the Spider Queen

Chaos has come to the Underdark
like never before.

New York Times best-seller!

CONDEMNATION, Book III
Richard Baker

The search for answers to Lolth's silence uncovers only more complex questions. Doubt and frustration test the boundaries of already tenuous relationships as members of the drow expedition begin to turn on each other. Sensing the holes in the armor of Menzoberranzan, a new, dangerous threat steps in to test the resolve of the Jewel of the Underdark, and finds it lacking.

Now in paperback!

DISSOLUTION, Book I
Richard Lee Byers

When the Queen of the Demonweb Pits stops answering the prayers of her faithful, the delicate balance of power that sustains drow civilization crumbles. As the great Houses scramble for answers, Menzoberranzan herself begins to burn.

INSURRECTION, Book II
Thomas M. Reid

The effects of Lolth's silence ripple through the Underdark and shake the drow city of Ched Nasad to its very foundations. Trapped in a city on the edge of oblivion, a small group of drow finds unlikely allies and a thousand new enemies.

The Avatar Series

New editions of the event that changed all
Faerûn...and the gods that ruled it.

SHADOWDALE
Book 1 • Scott Ciencin

The gods have been banished to the surface of Faerûn,
and magic runs mad throughout the land.

TANTRAS
Book 2 • Scott Ciencin

Bane and his ally Myrkul, god of Death, set in motion a plot to seize
Midnight and the Tablets of Fate for themselves.

The New York Times *best-seller!*
WATERDEEP
Book 3 • Troy Denning

Midnight and her companions must complete their quest by traveling
to Waterdeep. But Cyric and Myrkul are hot on their trail.

PRINCE OF LIES
Book 4 • James Lowder

Cyric, now god of Strife, wants revenge on Mystra, goddess of Magic.

CRUCIBLE: THE TRIAL OF CYRIC THE MAD
Book 5 • Troy Denning

The other gods have witnessed Cyric's madness
and are determined to overthrow him.

The original Chronicles

From *New York Times* best-selling authors Margaret Weis & Tracy Hickman

These classics of modern fantasy literature -- the three titles that
started it all -- are available for the very first time in individual
hardcover volumes. All three titles feature stunning cover art
from award-winning artist Matt Stawicki.

DRAGONS OF AUTUMN TWILIGHT
Volume I
Friends meet amid a growing shadow of fear and rumors of war.
Out of their story, an epic saga is born.

DRAGONS OF WINTER NIGHT
Volume II
Dragons return to Krynn as the Queen of Darkness launches her assault.
Against her stands a small band of heroes bearing a new weapon:
the DRAGONLANCE.

DRAGONS OF SPRING DAWNING
Volume III
As the War of the Lance reaches its height, old friends clash amid
gallantry and betrayal. Yet their greatest battles lie within each of them.